PYTHON'S
KISS

ALSO BY LOUISE ERDRICH

LOUISE ERDRICH

PYTHON'S KISS

STORIES

corsair

CORSAIR

First published in the United States in 2026 by HarperCollins
First published in Great Britain in 2026 by Corsair

1 3 5 7 9 10 8 6 4 2

Designed by Elina Cohen
Snake pattern © Andrei Chudinov / Shutterstock
Illustrations by Aza Erdrich Abe

A CIP catalogue record for this book
is available from the British Library.

Hardback ISBN: 978-1-4721-6081-2
Trade Paperback ISBN: 978-1-4721-6082-9
ANZ Trade Paperback ISBN: 978-1-4721-6127-7

Printed and bound in Great Britain by Clays Ltd, Elcograf S.p.A.

Papers used by Corsair are from well-managed forests
and other responsible sources.

Corsair
An imprint of
Little, Brown Book Group
Carmelite House
50 Victoria Embankment
London EC4Y 0DZ

The authorised representative
in the EEA is
Hachette Ireland
8 Castlecourt Centre,
Dublin 15, D15 XTP3, Ireland
(email: info@hbgi.ie)

An Hachette UK Company
www.hachette.co.uk

www.littlebrown.co.uk

To Aza
Who had a vision for each story

CONTENTS

PYTHON'S KISS

He was the second, or perhaps the third, Nero owned by my grandparents. With a grocery store that included a butcher shop and a slaughterhouse, they could feed as many dogs as they liked. Nero, a mixture of fierce breeds in a line known locally as guard dogs, was valued for his great strength, his formidable jaws, and his resonant bark. At night, he was turned loose to guard the cash register in the front of the shop, where he paced the waxed linoleum, a ghostly white. Other unbanked valuables were kept in a safe, but that was in my grandfather's bedroom. He slept behind a locked door with my grandmother on one side and a loaded gun on the other. This was not a place where a child got up at night to ask for a glass of water.

I was taken to stay with my grandparents because my mother was about to have a baby. The plan was for me to stay there until the baby was established at home—a period of only two or three weeks. While there, I must have lived at a more intense pitch. Or perhaps the novelty of everything that happened caused each day to imprint itself deeply on my mind. I believe I can still draw the stippled print on my grandmother's homemade dresses, or even reproduce the maps of blood that appeared and disappeared on my grandfather's bleached, starched, ankle-length aprons. I was eight years old, wore boys' clothes, and was often mistaken for a boy, a skinny one. Don't you feed him? the customers would say, laughing. My grandfather stopped giving me jobs out front. Every day, I climbed the trestle fence to watch Uncle Jurgen, lean in steel-toed boots, bring pigs, sheep, even steers and heifers, into a stilled submission. My grandfather, a real wrestler, had taken prizes in Germany. But Jurgen had his own ways. He grappled with each animal without exerting, it seemed, much effort. When the animal had tired itself out and stopped kicking, he'd use a razor-sharp knife to cut its throat with a technique so precise that the blood could be collected for black sausage.

Now the scalding tub for pigs is rusted, thistles have grown through the wire chicken cages, and somewhere in the field behind the closed shop, the bones of Nero whitely petrify.

THROW DOWN THE guts when he rushes at you, my grandmother said, handing me a bent pie tin heaped with offal. Nobody argued with her, ever. Sometimes Nero buried his dishes in the fenced backyard after emptying them or, if acutely bored, tossed them high in the air with his great muzzle. He caught these objects and chewed them to lethal shreds of metal, which littered the ground, along with his dung, and had to be picked up by one of the old men who worked odd jobs in exchange for schnapps. As instructed, I threw down the guts and backed away. Nero snapped down his food and stared at me. His eyes were nobly set in his broad brow. I stepped behind the screen door, but Nero held my gaze.

As I looked into his eyes, which were the same brownish gold as mine, I had my first sensation of self-awareness. I realized that my human body, my human life, was arbitrary. I could have been a dog. An exhilarating sadness gripped me, and then I felt the first intimations of sympathy for another form of creation, for Nero, who had to eat guts from an old pie tin. In the kitchen, there was a ceramic cookie jar in the shape of a fat baker. It was always filled with gingersnaps that had gone stale in the shop. The jar was on top of the rounded, plump-looking refrigerator, but was easily reached if I stood on the table. I took two cookies to the back door, opened it a crack, and tossed one of them toward Nero. He caught it with a jump. He caught the second one too. After that, it became my custom to take a few gingersnaps to the door and toss them to Nero, in the spirit of secretly aiding a fellow prisoner. For I had a confused sensation that we were both captive—in different bodies, true, but with only one dark way out.

EVERY ANIMAL HAD its use. Most, of course, were there to be slaughtered or, in the case of chickens and guinea hens, to lay eggs and then be slaughtered. The smaller dogs were there to keep my grandparents' feet warm and to accompany them on deliveries. They were given a few pats and scratches, but Nero, as a guard dog, wasn't treated with human affection. Therefore he never begged, wagged his tail, smiled with his tongue lolling, or pricked up his ears with excitement at certain words. He knew no human words except the one I taught him: gingersnap. The only sign of his understanding was a keener look in his eyes, a stiller stillness, a slight crouch for the midair catch. But it is probably impossible for our two species, interdependent since the dim beginning of our ascendancy on this earth, not to communicate. Staring at each other, we were exchanging some signal. After being fed or catching his daily gingersnaps, Nero trotted away to lie underneath a rogue pine that had grown up close to the door. When his food was digested, he usually returned to his primary daytime task—attempting to break out of the backyard.

It was well-known that Nero was not just looking for freedom. He was infatuated with a mean snub-nosed cocker spaniel named Mitts. She lived on the other side of the fairgrounds with Priscilla Gamrod, the shop's bookkeeper. Mr. Gamrod owned a bar and was known to fling men twice his size out his door by their collar and belt. Priscilla was twenty-five, but she still lived with him. Her mother had died, leaving the two of them bound by a grief that eased with time but was replaced by Mr. Gamrod's jealous dependence. This had got so bad that he insisted on fighting any man who tried to court her. He'd beaten them all, and Priscilla had put up with it because she hadn't found a man she liked yet anyway. Priscilla doted on Mitts and took her everywhere, brushed and beribboned. Once a year, she bred Mitts to Lord Keith, a papered stud who lived on a farm near Long Prairie. She sold the purebred pups only to people who met her standards, and cried when the last one left the house. Nobody knew if Mitts preferred Lord Keith to Nero, because she bit every dog and person within her reach. Priscilla, with her bandaged fingers, often had to cope with Nero's longing, but she never called the town dogcatcher.

Every time Nero broke loose, Jurgen built the fence higher. He used a combination of materials—old pickets, long staves, chicken wire, and spare rebar. He had it up to seven feet now, but the haphazard nature of its construction made the outcome almost certain; there were always bits of wood or metal jutting out on which Nero could gain purchase. For a couple of days now, he had been practicing his ascent. Over and over, he rushed at the fence, each time gaining a few inches of height. From one side of the yard to the other, using subtle variations in each approach, Nero strove. He kept at this the entire afternoon and could be heard before dawn the next day, throwing himself upward.

When I read the words 'dogged pursuit,' I see the literal efforts of Nero. The grown-ups in the family were used to this and confident in the seven-foot fence, so I was the only one watching when Nero clambered to the rickety top, balanced, and leaped into space. It was early in the morning, and the shop was already busy, so in theory an entire day could elapse before Nero's services were required and his escape was discovered. I filled my pockets with gingersnaps, told my grandmother I was going to play out in the field, and went straight across the sleepy fairgrounds to Priscilla Gamrod's house.

When Priscilla answered the door, Mitts barked viciously and darted for my ankle, but Priscilla elegantly kicked her dog down the hall with the pointed toe of her shoe. Mitts rolled, skidded, and trotted sullenly before us into the kitchen. She slumped in her pillowed corner, glowering as only a cocker spaniel can glower, while Priscilla sat me at the table and warmed some sugared milk with a bit of coffee in a small blue pan. She also made me cinnamon toast. The kitchen table was white enameled steel, painted with swirling green lines. The chairs were of curved aluminum with fat plastic cushions, green too. The wallpaper was decorated with little black roosters.

When I told Priscilla that Nero had cleared the fence, she said that she had the hose ready and would give him the works. She said this affectionately and even glanced at Mitts with a sort of amused pride, as if her dog's attractions reflected upon her too, though she needed no help. Priscilla was sweet figured, silky skinned, rosy, with black curls and brilliant pixie eyes. The way her lashes curled, reaching nearly up to her curved brows, entranced me. Her eyes were a warm hazel. It was no wonder that her father fought off boy after boy. I said something about this without thinking.

Oh, you heard about that, she said, smiling. He'll have a hell of a time fighting off the man I'm seeing now!

I wanted to ask who this man was, but right then Mitts yapped. Priscilla looked out the window, and, sure enough, there was Nero. He stood gravely in the scraggle of grass and sand pickers that passed for a yard. I stepped out the back door. Gingersnap, I said. Nero's ears pricked up. I was elated. He knew me. He snatched cookies from the air while Priscilla made the phone call, then he turned, listened intently, and loped off. A moment later, my uncle pulled up in the shop's meat truck. I stepped into the kitchen and, it so happened, entered at an angle from which I could just see the front door. Priscilla opened it for my uncle, who kissed her with a fast, furtive gesture, locking his hand for a moment in her black curls.

My uncle was tall and spare, handsome only if you liked thin cheeks and big teeth. He had a protruding Adam's apple, bulging temples, big ears. I didn't think he'd be any match for Priscilla's father. I was sure that their love was doomed and my uncle was likely to be killed or maimed.

Any coffee left?

Uncle Jurgen walked back into the kitchen, winked at me, then opened the refrigerator, which held half a frosted lemon layer cake. He grinned as Priscilla entered.

You'll have your cake and eat it too, she laughed.

As she cut the cake, she said, teasingly, Happy birthday to us. Jurgen reached down to pick up Mitts, who bit his hand. Instead of withdrawing his hand, my uncle stuck his fingers out and flicked her nose. He reached for her again. She bit him. He flicked her nose. This happened one more time, but the fourth time he reached for Mitts she didn't bite. She allowed him to pick her up and she sat across his thighs as he ate a piece of cake and scratched her long silky ears.

Uncle Jurgen said he'd have to spend the rest of the afternoon building the fence higher.

You should make sure you've got your dog back first, Priscilla said.

Oh, he won't go far. He's hung up on poor Mitts.

Poor Mitts? I said. She tried to bite off your fingers!

My uncle laughed and held up his hand. His long, thin fingers were heavily callused.

Mitts' teeth can't dent this hide, he said. He stroked the dog's throat, scratched her chin, and made soft clicking noises with his tongue. Mitts looked at him with wet, adoring eyes.

Priscilla took his plate to the sink. While her back was turned, Jurgen nudged me and nodded at the door. I went outside to sit on the back porch. They talked low for a while, laughed, and then Uncle Jurgen called out that I could catch a ride back with him. The warm truck smelled of scorched foam rubber, smoked sausages, and stale cigars. On the way, he told me that he had plans to marry Priscilla Gamrod. He'd asked her and she'd said yes.

Won't you have to fight her father? I asked.

Jurgen said he wasn't worried. I was too shy to disagree with an adult out loud, but what muscles my uncle had were thin and ropey. He even had a slight stoop. Mr. Gamrod stood upright as a fireplug, and his muscles were thick and hard.

At my grandparents' house, I helped my uncle carry some odds and ends of wood to the backyard so that he could add another foot or so to Nero's fence. Jurgen stood on top of the stepladder.

This is as far as I can work without buying an extension ladder, he said. And I'm saving for a ring.

The fence was now close to eight feet. When Nero finally turned up, hungry for his supper, I was disappointed that he hadn't kept on running, found his way up north, and joined a wolf pack.

A COUPLE OF days later, there was an explosion in the bookkeeping office. Not the usual explosion, which was of papers—toppling stacks, tipping files. This explosion involved a lot of shouting and swearing as Mr. Gamrod strode around the counter and into the office, where Priscilla was writing out invoices.

I was helping my grandmother unpack boxes to restock the cleaning-supply section with glossy cardboard containers of Comet and bars of Lava soap. Uncle Jurgen and my grandfather were out on a delivery. When the yelling commenced, my grandmother rushed to the office, slippers flapping, and stood for a moment in the doorway with her hands on her hips.

Psia krew!

My grandmother was the daughter of a Polish coal miner, and her one curse, rarely uttered, always silenced the Germans.

Mr. Gamrod held out the wedding-announcement page from the local newspaper. My grandmother took it from him and read it.

You coulda told us, she said to Priscilla, then nodded at Mr. Gamrod. They coulda told us.

Mr. Gamrod, happy to take on a sense of hurt indignation along with his own fury, nodded soberly.

Suddenly, there were tears in my grandmother's hard eyes. As we all stood immobilized by those tears, we heard Uncle Jurgen and my grandfather drive to the back entrance. The truck's motor quit, and there was a slide of suspense. They entered the house and came down the hall talking casually, but when they saw us they stopped.

My grandmother rammed herself toward Jurgen and pushed the paper into his chest. She continued down the hall without speaking. We heard the door to the sacred bedroom slam, the dead bolt thwock.

Well, Mr. Announcement Page, Gamrod said to Jurgen, rolling up his sleeves. When's it going to be?

You'll fight me first, my grandfather said. His sleeves were already rolled up and his thick forearms bulged. Everyone knew about his prize wrestling, but also that he had a touchy heart.

If Gamrod needs a fight, I'll fight, Jurgen said. He folded his gangly arms, with the cuffs of his blue plaid shirt neatly buttoned. Even I could tell that the statement was made with a certain irony, pointing out the absurdity of Mr. Gamrod's challenge.

Daddy, Priscilla said. I could've run away! She shook her black curls at her father and cradled Mitts, whose eyes rolled toward Jurgen.

All of a sudden, Nero set up a quavering high howl from the back-yard. His howling was a liquid gargle that mesmerized us until my grandmother opened the bedroom door and shouted at me to run out and throw a bucket of water on the damn dog.

I went into the kitchen and took all the gingersnaps out of the jar. Then I stood in the backyard tossing them to Nero. I ate a couple too. By the time they were gone, the Gamrods had left and my grandparents and my uncle were sitting in the kitchen, drinking beer and eating slices of summer sausage with dill pickles and rye bread. They were discussing the upcoming fight between Jurgen and Mr. Gamrod. It turned out that they'd agreed to host this fight out in the back field, where there was a sandy spot. They'd meet around dusk. The spectators would bring flashlights. Because the fight was on private property, shielded from the road, it probably wouldn't draw the police. Something in the calm and even good-natured way they discussed the upcoming battle, their laughter at how Mr. Gamrod had roared in, should have reassured me.

DURING MY FIRST full year of school, a lyceum show had been held in the school gym. This show, one of many small educational perfor-mances that toured our state, had had a powerful impact on me. The subject was dangerous exotic creatures. It was not a slideshow or a movie; this performance featured the animals themselves.

The man who ran the show had a confident air and a polished, domelike head. He was probably called Mr. Johnson, like so many men in the Midwest. He wore a gray three-piece suit and had a young Burmese python draped over his shoulders. He seemed to feed on our shocked murmuring as he proudly carried the patterned bronze loop of muscle to an open blue suitcase. He laid the snake inside and low-ered the lid. From another case, he removed a large jar with enough white sand in the bottom to bury a tarantula. Sure enough, when he opened the jar and set it down on its side, an enormous black spider tiptoed out. Miss Sillet, the fourth-grade teacher, fainted in her chair. None of the children noticed. Mr. Johnson had removed a soft plume from his vest.

A feather is the only thing that should ever be used to coax along a tarantula, Mr. Johnson said. They do not like to be poked.

As he brushed the tarantula along, encouraging it to climb the leg of his pants, he described how tarantulas use their long fangs to inject paralyzing venom into their prey. He explained how this venom liquefied the insides of insects, rodents, even small birds. The spiders sucked out this inner soup, leaving only the creature's husk. He told us that tarantulas could live to be thirty years old. The spider paused at his belt and then tested the cloth of Mr. Johnson's sleeve. It continued climbing, with only the lightest touches from the feather, until it was poised on Mr. Johnson's shoulder. There were gasps as its eerily jointed black legs used the tip of Mr. Johnson's ear to ascend. Once it reached the top of Mr. Johnson's head, the tarantula braced its awful legs and lowered its abdomen. There it rested. We were riveted. Mr. Johnson told us that the bite of a tarantula is no more dangerous to a human than a bee sting, but we didn't believe him. After a few minutes, he slowly tipped his head, signaling to the tarantula that it was time to make its way back down his body to the jar of sand. But just as the tarantula was testing the cuff of his trouser leg, all hell broke loose.

The lid popped up on the blue suitcase. The young snake writhed through the air like living electrical current and connected with Mr. Johnson. The jolt, as it threw its coils around Mr. Johnson's hips, sent the tarantula spinning like a flailing discus. When the spider hit the ground, it rose to show its fangs and danced aggressively to the front of the stage. In the meantime, Mr. Johnson was trying to stave off the snake's crushing hug. All this occurred just as his two assistants, plus the janitor and our gym teacher, Miss Oten, were carrying in what was supposed to be the show's grand finale, the African rock python.

They were bringing it down the aisle in the longest carrying case I'd ever seen. It was specially made of leather, with mesh windows through which the snake's mottled bulk could be glimpsed. The front of the case had been opened so that all the children could behold the spectacular somnolent indifference of the python's face. But we barely noticed it—we were watching Mr. Johnson. His snake had got the wrap on him and was squeezing tighter with every breath. Mr. Johnson had fallen to the stage floor and was kicking the boards resoundingly, with useless desperation, and not even the air to yelp. The tarantula had stopped prancing about on its hind legs and now picked its way down the side of the stage, away from the dangerous vibrations and toward the screaming children. At that point, the four people carrying the long python case dropped it and rushed to the assistance of Mr. Johnson. They vaulted onto the stage and were trying to pry Mr. Johnson free when the python glided into the mob of children.

Like many of the children, I was now standing on my chair. The cheap tin folding chairs were rickety, and others crashed right and left. The teachers didn't know what to do—they were picking children up, shoving them toward the doors, and trying to revive Miss Sillet. One was using a collapsed chair to hold off the tarantula. The python slid among the chair legs, and, as if in a nightmare, I fell directly before it. I looked straight into its impartial, primordial face. Its tongue flickered, sensing the currents of pandemonium, and then the forked tip touched me just above my upper lip, on the right cheek. That's all. It did not open its jaws to try to swallow me whole. It moved away.

I headed back to my classroom. The python had, what, tasted me, scented me? Kissed me? The touch of its tongue had been dry and lighter than the stroke of a sable paintbrush. Yet the touch left me with a vast feeling I have yet to name. It was more than a sensation. It was as though I had been chosen—marked for wisdom or maybe sorrow. Or perhaps, I think now, a sense of the ridiculous in these extremes of experience. I veered off to the school bathroom and looked in the mirror, but there was no sign. Anyway, it was the boa constrictor that dominated my impressions the night that Uncle Jurgen fought Mr. Gamrod.

MY GRANDFATHER DREW a ring in the sand and directed the men with flashlights to position themselves just outside the wide circle. That afternoon, I had gone out to the field and cleared the area of sand pickers. The spectators were mostly in favor of Mr. Gamrod's showing a certain leniency. There was talk of not being too harsh on the young man, of cutting him up just a bit, of doing only small damage to his face. He needs all the good looks he can keep, some-one laughed.They were telling Mr. Gamrod to have his fun but not go overboard. Mainly, they were worried that Priscilla would show up.

Mr. Gamrod divested himself of his shirt. He handed it delicately, by the tip of its collar, to his beer supplier and asked the man to hold it carefully so as not to ruin Priscilla's starching. Uncle Jurgen already wore a T-shirt and a pair of old dungarees. Both men went barefoot and gloveless. I thought Jurgen was keeping his T-shirt on so as not to reveal his skinny physique, but it turned out he had another reason. Mr. Gamrod instructed Jurgen to cry quit, or signal quit if he couldn't speak. The spectators laughed when Jurgen said, Likewise. This was supposed to be a fight to submission, although the fact was it could be stopped at any time by my grandfather. Or, if my grandmother were to charge across the field and yell her Polish curse—it would most certainly stop then. So I was allowed to stay. Jurgen even argued for it. I stood spellbound at my grandfather's hip.

Dukes up, head down, Mr. Gamrod advanced. His face darkened as he searched out an opening for the punch he would use to knock Jurgen out. That was the plan I'd heard from Gamrod myself. *I'll show mercy, all right—one punch should do it.* A shudder rose in me at the look of him with his barbell-trained muscles. He was Mad Dog Vachon—a neckless peg of hairy power. But Jurgen was no Verne Gagne—the straight-arrow champion TV wrestler of those days. He edged out with his fists raised, too, but instead of hopping around he studied Mr. Gamrod with an infuriating professorial air that had no place in the sandy ring. Mr. Gamrod hopped closer, punched the air, as if to test it, then slammed forward to connect his famous left hook. But Jurgen ducked. In fact, he not only ducked but in a bizarre blur folded his gangly body into a ball, rolled behind Mr. Gamrod, and came back up with an air of calm readiness. Mr. Gamrod whirled, his eyes narrowed, and he charged. Again Jurgen slid from his fists— this time to the far side of the ring. *Badapuckpuck!* Someone made chicken noises. A smile creased Mr. Gamrod's face, the flashlights flickered, and I thought my uncle was finished. Mr. Gamrod plunged at Jurgen and managed to grab hold of his T-shirt so that he could punch him. But after a bit of thrashing about, the punches always missing their target, Jurgen was out of the shirt and had neatly wrapped Mr. Gamrod's arms together with it. Gamrod managed to pull away.

It was what happened next that brought the Burmese python to mind. Jurgen moved. But to say he simply moved doesn't capture it. He moved the way that that snake had flung itself from the unlatched case. He was one long stream of electric, muscular motion that connected beneath Mr. Gamrod's fists. A twist of Jurgen's long leg behind Gamrod's solid calf and the two continued onward, borne down into the sand. Mr. Gamrod was a wrestler also, known for his early years as a Greco-Roman grappler on the college circuit. So it was no surprise when he flipped Jurgen on his back and seemed to pin him down, but as this was not a regular wrestling match, with score-keeping, Jurgen would have to signal for the match to be over.

It was over in the minds of most of the flashlight holders. A few yelled out that Jurgen was beat. But my grandfather reminded everyone of the rules. In the meantime, Jurgen had wrapped his legs around the bulging mound of Mr. Gamrod, hooking his ankles into the small of Gamrod's back. Perhaps Gamrod was feeling claustrophobic. With an enormous groan of effort, he reared back and tried to punch Jurgen in the head, but Jurgen now pressed his legs together even more tightly, pulling Gamrod down again. This time you could see Gamrod didn't want to be pulled down. His eyes rolled. He struggled the way Mr. Johnson had struggled. Jurgen's legs, arms, and feet were constantly manuevering Mr. Gamrod, squeezing at him, positioning him. I thought of the many animals that Jurgen had subdued. Every time Mr. Gamrod strained against him, Jurgen used that energy to his own advantage. He was exhausting Gamrod, pacifying Gamrod, letting Gamrod know what the animals eventually knew: Jurgen was inevitable. His arms were clasped, tight as a drowning child's, around Gamrod's neck. Jurgen's eyes were clear, dispassionate. He wasn't breathing hard, though his face was suffused with color. He was simply waiting for Mr. Gamrod's dizziness to turn into amazement and for Mr. Gamrod to beat his arm on the sand when he understood that his amazement could turn to death.

Mr. Gamrod struck his arm on the ground. Jurgen slid from under him. He stood and helped Priscilla's father to a wobbly crouch. Then Priscilla herself elbowed in through the circle of men and stood there, holding Mitts. She bent over, made sure her father was all right.

There's meatball hot dish still warm in the oven, Dad, she said. I'll be home late. Get some sleep. She took Jurgen's arm, and they walked about fifty paces before confronting Nero.

Aw, not you, Jurgen said to the dog.

A length of rope dangled from Nero's collar and he didn't growl when Jurgen picked it up.

It's time to let him loose in the shop, anyway, Jurgen said. He walked him into the store, tossed in a couple of dried-up wieners, and locked up. He and Priscilla left me there too, in my grandparents' house, and walked off to plan their new life.

THE NEXT MORNING, Jurgen stared at the fence a long time before leaving in the truck. He returned with a roll of wire and the equipment to attach it to the top of the fence. He tinkered around with the spot on the side of the house where the electrical current fed in from the power pole. He was on the ladder all the rest of the morning, carefully threading the wire. He wouldn't let me near. Nero rested in the shadow of the pine tree.

It was noon by the time Jurgen had finished and flipped the breaker. My grandfather closed up the shop for an hour and each had a beer as they watched from the kitchen windows. It took no time at all. Nero launched himself, scrambled up the fence exactly the way he'd puzzled out the day before. When the electrified wire touched him, he yelped like a puppy and fell, twisting. He lay still a moment, then rose and began to walk in wobbly, widening circles, until he reached the other side of the yard. He stood, panting, then suddenly gathered himself and bounded forward. Again Nero made his peculiar way up the fence, only this time when he reached the wire he snatched it between his teeth before he fell.

Nero shorted out the lights in the house and in the display cases, the fridge, the freezers, and everything else that didn't run off the generator. Then he lay on the ground with the dead cord beside him.

My grandparents and uncle ran around madly trying to restore the power. I went to Nero. He was still breathing. I sat down next to him, and for the first time put my hands on him. I stroked his forehead and scratched behind his ears. When at last he could rise, he dragged himself to the corner of the yard and curled up in the rust-colored pine needles, his nose hidden in his tail. I watched over him for the rest of the afternoon. He was beautiful, like a white wolf in the forest. I didn't want to be human anymore.

MR. GAMROD COULD not stop talking about his trip to the other world. To Priscilla, to my grandparents, to the patrons of the bar, and to anyone else who would listen, he would describe how in the clutch of Jurgen's limbs he had died and come to life again. He had not walked into the light. He had not seen Jesus. The only way he could explain it was to say that he had been suspended in a timeless present that held the key to . . . something. He'd felt his arm pound the earth just as he was about to grasp the meaning of it. A few days later, he realized he was no longer afraid. After death he would understand the answers to questions that in this life he couldn't even put into words. Aside from this new assurance, Mr. Gamrod didn't seem much changed.

I didn't get to see the change in Nero, either. He was still quietly recovering when I left, sleeping long days in the pine needles. I went home to my new baby brother.

SIX MONTHS OR so passed before we returned for a Christmas visit. It hadn't snowed for weeks, and the ground was covered with what midwesterners call snirt. Everything was gray and grainy, like a blurred old movie. Nero no longer lived in the backyard but in a cage constructed out of the chicken run. The wire had been replaced with a thicker grade and it even ran beneath the ground, Jurgen said. The chicken-wire roof, which had once foiled hawks, now kept Nero from jumping out.

It was one thing to walk out the back door into the yard where Nero lived. It was another thing entirely to walk into his cage. He seemed more dangerous now. His coat had yellowed. He didn't recognize me. I had become one of the betrayers. He didn't come forward for a gingersnap, didn't even notice the cookies I threw onto the trampled shit-strewn dirt. He was obsessed with an old iron cauldron, which he flipped up and down with jerks of his massive head. He wrestled with it. Rolled it, bit at it. He was raw energy with just one focus.

It was early summer the next time we visited. Nero was losing his winter coat, and clumps stuck out in filthy puffs. He was still rolling his cauldron around but now with only stubs of teeth—he'd broken them on the iron. Jurgen no longer took Nero out to guard the shop. My uncle still worked there but was married to Priscilla now, living several blocks away. My grandparents had installed an electrical alarm system.

One day, with no word to anyone, Jurgen went to the chicken run and shot Nero. I was standing outside with nowhere to go when I saw him hauling the dog to the back field, by his tail, like a scrap of rug. He carried a shovel. I grabbed another. Together we dug deeply into the ground. We lowered Nero down as far as our arms could reach. Then, along with something of myself, we dropped him into the timeless present.

I have seen him there many times in this long life.

WEDDING DRESSES

During a January thaw, water trickled from a burst pipe down an interior wall, into a basement storage closet, and ruined all of Dora's wedding dresses. There was the perfect knee-length dress with transparent sleeves sewed from a Vogue pattern. There was the ecru ribbon skirt and shawl trimmed with appliqué flowers from Dora's guess-again marriage—to a traditional man who played moccasin games. Then there was her green brocade dress with a beaded belt of indigo swallows. That marriage had not been legally recognized, but she counted it. And at last a heavy white satin dress with forty covered buttons up the back, a kick train, and a bodice trimmed with swirling sea creatures beaded of tiny pearls. This was from a vintage store and cost six hundred dollars, a purchase Dora had pondered for quite a while. All of the dresses were soaked and perhaps rotted, alive with pink-green bubbles of mold.

The leak had been stealthy and when she finally discovered it and opened the basement closet, she became more upset than the situation warranted—after all, they were just dresses she would never wear again. Just as she would never be married again. She had determined upon that. It wasn't the loss of the actual dresses, she thought, it was their squalid disintegration that was so disturbing. Memories of her marriages had been dry and controlled. When she moved the hangers, she released a cloud of choking spores—as if she'd exposed a dead thing, a moldy growing thing moving with avidly feeding alien lives.

She turned off the water to the kitchen sink pipe and cleaned up the mess, hunched over, whimpering softly as she used a water glass to trap an eerily prancing house spider. The spider had crept into soggy folds of satin and set up a webby burrow. At the time, she was taking care of Martha, her eleven-year-old niece. Martha was always an eager participant in spider trappings, and was at Dora's elbow when she released it into the snow.

'Will it freeze?'

'No,' said Dora. 'Look.'

Already the spider was creeping down the side of the house, back into the basement. Martha patted Dora's hand and took the water glass. Dora told her niece that she was sorry for making pathetic noises.

'Auntie. Your wedding dresses were wrecked.'

Martha said this as though it was self-evident that her aunt should be upset, and Dora let herself feel something, a twinge. The only mainstream bridal dress was the one with the stylized starfish and snails, so whimsical on a wedding dress. But the others had been made by relatives, and by Dora, gossiping and listening and giving advice while they worked. Her mother or one of her sisters presided at a sewing machine at the head of a kitchen or dining room table. Dora washed out the water glass, muttering.

'I think it was the aliveness. How the dresses had turned into something like . . .'

'Cheese?'

'More alive than cheese. They were, like, bride gowns for zombies.' Martha said this with a hint of pride at her idea.

'You're so right.'

'Can we have Chinese food?'

To Martha, her aunt's derangements were occasions for shrimp fried rice and lemon chicken. Dora and Martha usually drove over to the Rainbow and looked forward to its comforts. Breathing the mold had made Dora dizzy, and she told Martha they'd go but she needed her body to catch up with her unexpected emotions. Martha gave a wise, womanly nod. Dora lay down on her bed, which was just the way she liked it, both firm and sinkingly soft. Martha flopped down too.

'I am reading *Lord of the Flies*.'

'Do they still teach that? I'm sorry, honey.'

Martha moaned with satisfaction at the drama. 'I have to do ten pages a night. You want me to read aloud to you?'

Dora pulled a comforter around the two of them and listened to Martha read in her competent, sensible, eleven-year-old voice. Piggy still didn't know what would happen. The beaded starfish were still okay, Dora thought. They could be sliced from the slimy mass of satin once it stiffened. All the dresses were in garbage bags, freezing on the back porch. Tomorrow she'd have to fix the pipe.

Dora sat up. 'I'm okay. We should go.'

'Wait a second.'

Martha put the book down. She gave her aunt a calm look from under her brown bangs. Her eyes were deep, dark, and so warm and questing that Dora and her sister, Bonnie, agreed it was easy to get lost in them. Bonnie was on a short marriage-maintaining trip with her husband, Jeke. They were probably going to be okay because they did take these trips. Martha had brothers, but they were with an uncle who had boys. Martha gave Dora a pang sometimes. Should she have had a child? Perhaps a daughter of her own? She was an outlier, the only one of her siblings who hadn't reproduced. She had borne the continual intrusive questions. Even her most feminist Native friends had said things like 'for the good of our people.' But she'd never wanted children of her own. Besides, no child could be as perfect as Martha, and she was perfect because Dora didn't have to do things like make and enforce rules. Dora could just listen to and dote on Martha. Dora hoped that Martha would stay this person through the soon-approaching age of twelve, and that when she got her promised cell phone, then fizzed up with hormones, she would be spared the worst. Dora also hoped that the sight of her moldered wedding dresses, spiders dancing in the satin folds, wouldn't blight Martha's relationships.

'Wait,' said Martha again.

'Wait for what?'

'I have a question. What do those wedding dresses, you know, like, stand for?'

'Stand for? They're just dresses.'

'But there's four dresses. Four weddings? Four marriages?'

'Right. I mean, a couple of the actual weddings were very small, only the witness basically.'

This was suddenly like being a real parent. Having to explain her own past to a child, and do it in a way that would have little impact, either negative or perhaps overly positive.

'So what was each one like? Why'd you marry them and why'd you split up?'

They were putting on their down puffer jackets—Dora's was black and Martha's bright blue. Dora's brain was scrambling around, hunting for words or ideas. How to even start.

'So, the first one, with the see-through sleeves. What's the story?'

Vintage Vogue with Transparent Sleeves

She'd been married long ago in a far distant land to a chubby white man, in New York City, when there was still a vacant lot next to the Mayflower Hotel, the New York Coliseum dominated the west side of Columbus Circle with car and trade shows, when there was a fanciful lollipop building and no Trump Tower. They'd lived in a one-bedroom condominium kitty-corner from Lincoln Center, where he had a job managing group ticket sales. She was there to become an artist, but there wasn't much room in their apartment. In fact, she had left her wedding dress in storage at her parents' house.

Dora started out by getting a job in the museum shop at the Metropolitan Museum of Art. Her husband, Merritt, had bought their condominium with his inheritance and put it in both their names in case he died. He was very careful with money and they were truly in love, but when they both signed the deed and title he did say, 'I'm stupid to do this,' and it stuck in her mind. Everybody in his family, including the women, had weak hearts and died young. To counter his genetics he began to run every day—this began as soon as they moved to the city. Dora thought that living in a place bought as the result of his father's death was a constant reminder to Merritt of his own mortality. That seemed heavy. Still, they were happy and started out every morning together. They walked across the park to the museum and then he just kept running. In many ways, it was a promising, even glowing, life.

However, there was the question of what came next. Children weren't immediately in the picture—the heart thing plus her reluctance. She and Merritt had a great rapport. He was funny, and she'd been fooled by that into thinking he was like an Indian. Her family was funny, he was funny, but then she was suddenly so far away from her family. So what came next was where they would live—New York or Minneapolis—because the apartment wasn't forever, that was clear. It was surprisingly small. Merritt had an expansive wardrobe and a lot of running shoes. There was no place for her sewing machine, let alone a place to make art. She had a tiny table in the bedroom, where she worked on small drawings and paintings, which she pieced together into larger works that took up all of their walls. After two years Dora and Merritt were right on top of each other. The stuff on her tiny table overflowed onto the floor and took up one half of the bedroom. Merritt's clothing and shoes took up almost the entire large closet on the other side of the bedroom and ended up in tubbies and laundry baskets. They tried to keep the living and dining area clear enough to entertain—mostly Merritt's remaining family and a few friends from work—but eventually that also became too cluttered and it all felt overwhelming.

Twice in two years, she had saved enough money for a trip home to Minneapolis, but that wasn't enough and she grew miserably homesick, while, in that time, Merritt grew more comfortable in his job and in the city. He also got thinner. The thinner he became, the more his personality changed—from easygoing to tense, from honest to dishonest, from funny to sarcastic, from excitable to morosely excitable, from loving how she looked to complaining about how she looked. One day she said to him, 'I'm really unhappy with you,' and he'd screamed, then shouted, 'Your hair is everywhere. You shed like a dog. I'm going to chop it off while you're asleep.'

For a month, she locked him out of the bedroom and made him sleep on the couch they'd hauled up from the sidewalk, the torture slab they'd kept so as not to encourage guests. They filed for divorce. He bought her out of the condominium. She shipped her art to Minneapolis and had enough money to buy an entire house.

'Is it still your house?' said Martha.

'Yes,' Dora answered.

She had finished the story in the parking lot of the Rainbow. Martha was quiet for a moment, thinking the story over.

'You still have your house, your long hair, and now you're an artist.'

'It was because of sewing that dress at a table with my mom, aunties, sisters. They wouldn't let me get married without telling me how to get divorced. Some might call that cynical, but it was a huge help. So all in all,' said Dora, 'things turned out.'

Wedding Dresses

'What about Merritt?'

'I have no idea and don't care. He knew hair is power.'

What She Didn't Tell Martha

Merritt had promised Dora over and over that he loved her hair, that he wouldn't dream of cutting it, that the very idea horrified him. He understood that shedding hair was her reaction to stress. He was pathetically sorry. She'd let her guard down, then awakened a week later, a lazy Sunday morning, with her hair all over the bed, sheared off raggedly. He'd gone for his run. She had gathered up her two-foot-long clumps of hair and locked him out of the apartment. In his morning fury, he'd left his wallet and his bank cards behind. After pounding on the door for a while, he'd slept at his brother's house and on Monday morning she'd withdrawn half of their money, solicited lawyer advice from a friend she worked with, hired her friend's attorney, filed for a divorce, had groceries delivered, used their credit card to hire a company to pack up her art and her other things too. She changed the lock on the bedroom door and put all of Merritt's clothing in the living room. She let him back into the apartment a few days later but locked him out of the bedroom. In the middle of the night he scratched on the bedroom door. He was having the heart attack he'd dreaded.

She got him to the hospital and he had a second heart attack there, which he barely survived. His family blamed her in spite of their genetic problem. They helped him fight her for her half of the condo, which had already increased in value. She'd flown back to New York twice, her hair short and ragged because she was so mad she refused to get a decent cut. She finally did get half the money, and the last she'd heard he'd stopped running and gone into finance.

She thought he'd have another heart attack and die in his second wife's arms, but he didn't. He just became rich. By then, her hair had grown out.

THE RAINBOW'S ENTRANCE was dim and moody. A small shrine glowed red and there was a mirrored bar lined with colorful bottles of liquor. Dora and Martha stopped in front of the shrine, then walked toward a table behind the koi tank. They ordered their usual drinks—for Martha a Shirley Temple with all the trimmings (maraschino cherries, swords, monkeys, an umbrella). For Dora a glass of white wine, which she knew she wouldn't finish. The drinks came and they ordered their usual food. They stared at the koi tank. Dora's heartbeat slowed. The glorious fish flared side to side.

Dora said, 'So much intelligence in their sleek bodies.' The kois' instinctive grace, dramatic and innocent, reminded her of how she'd been back then but hadn't known. She saw herself walking through the mottled light on leafy paths through Central Park, her long dark hair swinging to her waist. It had never grown that long again. Past the fish, they watched wavery figures raising chopsticks to their lips.

'What about the next dress?' said Martha.

'Really? You're not satisfied?'

'There wasn't *that* much drama.'

'You watch too much *Real Housewives*.'

'No way. Mom won't let me.'

'I'm stalling for time.'

'Just tell me, quick.'

Wedding Dresses

Ecru Ribbon Dress and Appliqué Flower Shawl

He courted her over cherry wine and touched her for the first time with the tail of his long braid, brushing it across her lips, which she thought of later as creepy. Dora didn't tell Martha about all of that, exactly, but said he was extremely romantic. He had adored her, healing her womanhood, she'd thought—embarrassing to remember now. She didn't say that to Martha either. His name was Johnny Ermine and he was Plains Ojibwe, Ho-Chunk, Cree, and Sioux Valley Sioux, Dakota, just a bit. He called his Dakota side his pepper and his OjiCree side his salt, as in salt of the earth. Dora's family had always thought the Cree were grumpy people— 'Likewise,' he said, laughing, when she told that to him. Johnny Ermine charmed everyone with his happy-go-lucky, friendly ways. He'd already had two wives; he was one up on her and he was just in his thirties. He swore, however, that she was his first and last. He had children already, so she felt she was off the hook. After only two months he asked her to marry him. Their sex life felt fated and was ever more intense. How far could it have gone? she wondered, watching the glamorous koi. Johnny Ermine had been so sweet on her that thoughts of having a child with him sometimes crept in.

'Hey, earth to Auntie,' said Martha.

'We got married up in Canada,' Dora said. 'My family sewed my dress and we caravanned up there. Johnny's reserve had a big round house. That's where we had the whole ceremony, the works, and the tribal judge signed off on the papers. We had some trouble about our clans because we were both fish clan, but we consulted the shake tent and found out his was sturgeon and mine was catfish, basically, which disappointed me, I'll be honest, because now I couldn't eat fried cat-fish. So a strike against us from the first. We lived up there for a summer, then came down here like a couple of snowbirds. I had kept my house, so we lived here. He got in touch again with his Dakota roots and started upping his moccasin-game gambling strategies with his guy friends, staying out late, but I had your mom and my cousins, so everything was cool. I'm not a jealous person, but Johnny Ermine was a prize, a unicorn, being educated and having a job, plus traditional, and although he was skinny and hunchy and had small eyes, he didn't need to be handsome with all his blood quantum, not down here. He was so much Cree that his other quantums were tiny. He was so deeply into me that I didn't worry. He would take me to powwows and we'd walk around the booths, dance in the sweetheart dances; he'd wink at me when I watched him play moccasin games with his posse. He said I was his one and only, he loved everything about me—my art, my family, the way I cooked, and the way I slept so soundly.'

Martha left for the bathroom and Dora kept the story going in her head.

She didn't tell Johnny that her sound sleeping had once contributed to a traumatic haircut and that she now woke every few hours throughout the night. Awake while Johnny was still out, she'd mulled things over.

Especially in the Native professional worlds of the Twin Cities, everybody knew one another way too well. You couldn't swing a cat without someone reporting they'd heard a meow. Dora heard Johnny was seen at lingering lunches with Camille Davies, so she went straight to Camille and asked her. That's how her mother had told her to handle these things. 'Go to the woman. She'll tell you because if she's seeing him she wants you out of the way. If you go to the man, he doesn't know what he wants and will probably lie.'

So Dora set up coffee with Camille, who worked at a nonprofit, and was not from a local tribe, so she heard. They got some lattes and sat downstairs among the indoor trees at the IDS court, under filtered sunshine and tiny leaves, among bank managers and homeless dudes and networking ladies. Camille was all dressed up. She was wearing all the Native bling imaginable—it was an intertribal blur. She was a redhead, she was stacked, she wore five-inch heels, and Dora knew from her first words that Johnny Ermine was seeing a real live pretendian.

'Our bond is nonsexual, it's sacred,' Camille said. 'He's just listening to my dreams and giving me teachings. My great-grandmother was Windigo tribe.'

Dora made the sign of the cross, a reflex gesture because she didn't go to church, but the windigo wasn't mentioned in normal conversation and a whole tribe of them would end the world.

'Amazing,' she said. 'Where is your reservation?'

'I got adopted out because I'm so light,' she said.

'How did that happen with the Indian Child Welfare Act?'

'My mother signed off on all the papers.'

'Where is she from?'

'Nobody will tell me.'

'That's too bad. Are you seeing my husband in a romantic way?'

'Just, you know, sacred. Nonsexual,' Camille said.

By which Dora thought they were hot and heavy, but technically perhaps within a centimeter of ordinary consummation, and that was why it all felt so sacred. It turned out, however, that Johnny had been with Camille the entire time he and Dora were married.

Dora said nothing of this to Martha when she came back from the bathroom, just summed it up:

'He started liking a fake Indian and I just ditched him. It was too much.'

Anyway, their food came. Martha's lemon chicken. Dora's silky tofu with snow peas and forest mushrooms. While they ate with greedy jubilance, Martha asked about the belt beaded with indigo swallows. It wasn't with the dress, so where was it?

'This is delicious,' Dora said, her chopsticks moving fast. 'Don't ruin it.'

'After, then.'

'Eat your chicken.'

ON THE WAY home, through the exuberant winter streets of a Friday night, Martha asked again about the third dress and its belt with the beaded swallows. Where was that belt?

'In a box.'

'Can I see it?'

'As long as you don't ask about the wedding or anything. I'm over-loaded. I need a rest.'

'I promise.'

Dora asked her niece about her friends, whether there was any drama, if she'd been to any parties, if any of them had phones yet, what sorts of objects she was saving up for in Animal Crossing. This was an attempt to divert Martha, so they could simply watch a movie before bed and Dora could give her heart a rest. But when they walked into the house, Martha insisted on seeing the swallow belt. Dora patted her heart and took the wooden box out of her top dresser drawer.

'Here it is,' she said, draping the belt across a pillow. It was a tie belt, the loom beadwork sewn onto a strap of brain-tanned leather. It was exquisite beadwork, number 13 beads, the swallows swooping up and down across a pale strip of sky, one tiny pink bead out of place to honor the creator. Someone had a vision. Maybe it was part of someone's regalia or a special outfit. She'd bought it at a powwow before thinking she'd get married again. There was some blue in the green brocade. The belt had been the perfect touch.

'You can have it,' Dora said.

'Really?' Martha stroked the beads, her warm eyes doubting, hoping.

'Yes, you can have it, if you do one thing. Don't ask me about that marriage.'

Martha said she wouldn't and looked both awed and intrigued. She opened her mouth, shut it, opened it again, and said, 'I really love this belt but I want to know about that husband too.'

'Tough,' Dora said, smiling at her.

Indigo Swallows

Dora liked to drink wine with dinner. She rarely had more than a glass and didn't drink alone. Samuel drank more but nothing to worry about. He was a thoroughly kind black-haired man, a descendant-status White Earth man, with green eyes and beautiful callused hands. He was a small-time contractor, a storyteller, a salesman, an innocent, very loyal, and he worked out in a gym. He didn't drink at their wedding, which was a pipe ceremony, no papers. She'd never seen him drunk until they were married for a year. It crept up slowly. During that year, she was still drinking her one glass, and he was finishing the bottle every other night. Then every night. Another year went by. Some money came along. They went to Mexico three times and Italy once. Glorious. Every night he was finishing the bottle and now he was starting on another. She asked him to quit, to join AA, and he tried. The first time lasted a month. The following innumerable times each lasted months too. He never did stay in rehab or make a year sober and at last he went out of business.

In a painful passion to save his life she gave him an ultimatum. She'd leave him. She didn't want to leave him. She started going to Al-Anon, even though she knew she'd leave him if she went to those meetings. She was the only Native person in her group but it was okay—booze levels everyone. Now he was finishing the second and third bottles and staying up until dawn to finish the fourth. She found rum bottles he had hidden. The recycling was insane.

Sometimes she poured herself a glass to drain some of the bottle, but would end up crying as she poured her wine down the sink. She loved him, they had a special world they could enter, sometimes a drunk world, but a world apart. Sometimes when they were holding each other, she closed her eyes and saw the swallows they had both loved from their separate childhoods. The midnight blue swallows were diving off the tops of granaries or silos or river cliffs and slipping through the air, like everything beautiful that flashes through life and disappears.

She knew how this would unravel and so did he. They both knew every alcoholic has the same basic story. Maybe now she was in love with the alcohol, not Samuel, because most of the time now the alcohol was talking. But there were still flashes of Samuel. She knew it all. The gold of liver failure was coming up under his skin. No Native person gets through life without knowing these things. Many women would have stayed with Samuel because he was a genial drunk, never raging or mean. But he was sweating out the liquor night and day, a sour, earthen, coffin smell.

Once, she came home when he was trying to get sober and he had all the appliances on—fans, vacuum cleaner, television, AC in the winter, the Roomba spinning calmly through the downstairs like a lost earnest soul. He had everything running in order to block out the noises in his head. Another time, in winter, she found him underneath a tarp in the yard. She didn't want to watch him die. The best to hope for now was he'd die in rehab, but he said he'd rather die in open air. The alcohol didn't care either way. She left the alcohol, not him. She missed the man she married, but that man had dived off a granary roof and vanished forever.

AFTER MARTHA WENT to bed that night, taking the belt of swallows with her, Dora drank some valerian tea and felt herself sinking into grief over Samuel. She forced herself to go to bed and covered herself with the bear paw quilt that she and Samuel had wrapped around themselves at their wedding. She dreamed that the quilt tightened around her and she woke twisted in the sheets, gasping with fear.

THE NEXT DAY, in blazing sunny cold, Bonnie came to pick up Martha, who showed her the beaded belt. Bonnie gave Dora a serious look over Martha's head. They put their hands on their hearts at the same time. Of course Samuel was dead now, had been dead for three years. Bonnie and Martha drove off. Then Dora thawed the burst pipe entirely with a hair dryer. She replaced the pipe and figured out how, by winding the PVC with heat tape and stuffing the outer wall with more insulation, she could keep the pipe from freezing again. This took her all day Sunday. The black bags were still on the back porch. She couldn't get herself to throw them in the garbage. Not yet. Dora opened one of them and used a razor on the last dress, the creamy satin. She brought the beadwork inside and lay it on an old pillowcase. She then felt that she should make some gesture of commemoration toward the dresses—but she couldn't think of exactly what. She was not a very ceremonial person, but she had a cedar bush by the house and she had picked that medicine last summer. In the end, she rummaged around until she found the cedar.

Dora put some in a small cast-iron frying pan, lighted it, carried the pan to the back porch, and waved the smoke over the black garbage bags. Later that night, she went out to get the bags, but they were fixed to the frozen boards. She hadn't tied the bags shut. She could have pulled out the dresses, put them into new bags, and thrown them out. But she didn't want to come into contact with the dresses again. So she left them out there.

THE WORLD STAYED frozen. Reaching for ever more colorful terms, the weather reporter changed the system from Polar Vortex to the Arctic Hammer. Dora worked from home and didn't have to go out much. All day, the snow outside reflected an especially bright light into her house, perfect winter light, the best for making art. She had time to think. It was strange that she'd once had such intensely positive intimate feelings about the people she'd married, who had either died or gone on to have entirely separate lives. She thought those feelings were like the paper flower toys she used to buy—cubes or pellets that unfurled their petals in water. Ruining her wedding dresses, and Martha's curiosity about them, had the effect of unfurling all the flowers at once. She entered a mad streak of work so she could put the gorgeous damage out into the world.

THERE WAS ANOTHER thaw and Dora remembered the bags on the back porch. The world was brilliant with sunlight and dripping with crystal water. She put her parka on, went out, picked up the damp bags of wedding dresses, and dragged them down the back steps. She wasn't going to feel or think, just pitch them out. One bag thumped, heavy. Dora dropped both bags and backed away. The first bag rustled and then was still, as if the animal, which was obviously inside it, was deciding what to do. She stepped back and kept watch. Eventually, the bag rustled again and a disheveled skunk emerged. It walked down the steps, still a bit woozy with sleep, and then ambled wearily through a gap in the lattices beneath the porch.

Now the bags were halfway down the back porch, and she didn't want to move them again. They looked awful, like she'd pitched her trash out on the steps, but she didn't want to risk another skunk.

A FEW WEEKS later she was taking care of Martha again, supposedly because Martha wanted a sleepover. Dora suspected there was more. There was one wedding dress left to explain, after all, and Martha was a completist. She always finished her homework and was now relating in detail how she had persisted in decorating her entire Animal Crossing island. Dora had decided that she might as well get the last dress over with.

'Speaking of animals, there was a skunk in my wedding dress bag,' she told Martha.

'A cute skunk?'

'I guess he was cute. But skunks can bite.'

'And shoot their scent. Have you noticed how one thing leads to another?' Martha asked.

'I have noticed that.'

'Now you'll have to get a dog,' she suggested. 'To keep away the skunk.'

'But then I'd have to worry about a dog.'

'I'd take care of it.'

'I know you would. You have a special understanding for animals, dogs especially. Did you come over because you wanted to know about the fourth wedding dress?'

'What? Oh. I know about Roberta. I heard enough.'

'Why'd you come over then?'

'Because you see into my heart.'

'What?'

'My heart. You see into my heart.'

Dora couldn't react, at first, but at last she spoke.

'I think that's the best thing anybody ever said to me.'

'Oh, well, yeah. Can we have Chinese food?'

Beaded Sea Creatures

So she didn't have to talk about Roberta after all. Martha remembered that they were together and pretty much knew why they were now apart. But of course Martha didn't know how, too soon after Samuel, they'd met—at the installation of an art exhibit—how they'd done such satisfying work on the way each piece was displayed, on the labels, on the catalog, on the interactions between the pieces. Nobody knew how surprised they were to have found each other. Most people didn't know when they got married. Solid, cheerful, brainy, brown-haired, passionate Roberta had persuaded Dora to get married, but insisted they have only Bonnie, their witness, at their wedding dinner.

Roberta didn't move into Dora's house because she wanted to keep living with her son, JJ, in her own St. Paul apartment. Dora was again off the hook as far as children were concerned, but that wasn't the reason she adored JJ. He was a sublime little toddler with hilarious ways. However, she found as the months went on that she spent less and less time with JJ. She'd become so fond of him that this caused her a surprising amount of pain and became the source of conflict. He was almost four. Then he was five. Then she found out JJ didn't know they were married, and his father, whom Dora hadn't seen since the art exhibit, didn't know about the marriage either. And it went further. Roberta still hadn't told her family.

Wedding Dresses

And further still. She had sworn to Dora that she'd told all these people about their marriage and everyone was happy for them.

Now Roberta insisted that she was not ashamed, or uncomfortable, or ambivalent. She laughed at the mention of anything negative. For her reasons were positive, she insisted. Dora listened as Roberta told her that she wanted to be private with Dora, to keep her a delicious treasure, and also that there was something about Dora she couldn't get to, that was locked in a safe that Roberta wanted to crack, and Roberta suspected that this thing was trauma or grief and this wasn't all her fault.

Dora felt the walls, the furniture, the couch cushions, the dark windows moving in on her, the ceiling lowering, dials clicking, as Roberta went on and on about how she wanted to have something precious, safe, eternal, hers alone, and—this was the kicker—sacred.

When Roberta used the word 'sacred,' Dora said, 'I'm done.' But then she added, 'I'm not giving you a divorce. If this is so eternal and, how dare you use this word, "sacred," you won't mind.' Dora bolted out and ran down the stairs of Roberta's apartment, decided to avoid her from then on. To her sorrow, she would not be allowed to see JJ anyway. She screenshotted Roberta's wall-of-words texts and emails, never answered, sent back any papers she received, unsigned, and generally resisted anything from Roberta's side of the Mississippi.

DORA DECIDED TO sew the sea creatures into a larger canvas of beaded and collaged and collected textiles. After she'd pulled out the green brocade, she tossed the other dresses. It seemed she'd passed the last test. Only Samuel's memory had survived. One evening, when all the leaves were out, in the first heat of summer, Dora sat on her back porch and watched the skunk lead two babies out toward the woodpile.

Perhaps it was strange that, of her loves, the hopeless alcoholic would be the one she still mourned, and somehow couldn't live without. For she'd had the green dress cleaned and hung it in her hall closet. Not her bedroom closet—that was too close—but out in the hall, where Samuel could invisibly greet anyone who entered, even offer to pour them a drink, silently, graciously, in the self-serving act of an alcoholic host. It was because he'd fall asleep with a strand of her hair in his grasp. He'd throw himself at her feet not in drunkenness but in delight. It was because he had tried to get sober countless times and failed, but the trying was brave. It was because when he was at his lowest he still respected her, in his way, by sleeping out in the garage. Or he slept on the floor beside her bed. It was because he still chopped wood, fried eggs and hash browns for her breakfast, and they loved the same movies and books. They had watched old movies—*Blade Runner*, *The Fifth Element*, *Willow*, *Tombstone*, *Powwow Highway*—many times. It was because after all he was a person, and she was a person, and they were real; she'd raged at him, but he kept a peculiar kind of honor. He'd never lied to her, he had been true to her. Yet she'd left him to die beneath the I-94 overpass on a subzero night, alone, while she was warm in bed, and nothing in the world of 12-step slogans and the Minnesota rehab community could ever make that right.

Or so she felt in her lowest ebbs.

The last time she'd seen him was at the big intersection between the cathedral and Loring Park. One side of his face was swollen. She pulled around the corner and got out of her car. They sat on a bench and talked.

'Come back,' she said. 'You're going to die out here.'

He only shook his head and smiled, fewer teeth.

She lifted his cardboard sign to herself and read it through dry eyes. On the front was the usual plea for money. On the back he'd scrawled a tiny message to himself.

Wedding Dresses

Tell Dora to find my teeth

'What does this mean?' she'd nearly asked, but she knew he was just saying, as he had so many times, that her efforts were doomed and faintly ridiculous. So she'd just held his hand and waited until he rose and walked away to join the others disappearing across the grass.

THE HOLLOW CHILDREN

At the Tabor bar, around beer number four, the men sometimes got into history farming, trading stories of their antecedents' exploits and agonies. In the long ago, wheat prices had plunged and most of the bonanza farms had broken up. That was when their great-greats had bought the land. The men talked about old plagues, old equipment, old swaps of ownership, crops, land, and dire weather. John Pavlecky's great-grandmother, at the age of nine, had survived the blizzard of 1923 by burrowing into a haystack when the school bus didn't show up. Diz remembered his grandfather telling stories about an Uncle Ivek, who had also endured that blizzard, which was particularly lethal because it started on a misty and mild April morning. Around eight that morning, the bus had been almost full of children and headed toward the school, when out of the northwest a wind of sixty miles an hour dropped the temperature instantly to -20 and filled the air with a blistering-cold curtain of powder. Such a snow would blind your eyes and scour the features off your face.

Ivek was a farmer, a part-time schoolteacher, and one of the bus drivers. He was taking his turn behind the wheel. In the back of a school notebook, not long after the blizzard, he wrote about what happened.

IVEK WAS BOUNCING down the muddy road when the mist dissolved and he saw it—a boiling white mass rolling at him like annihilation. He drove straight in at full speed, hoping to make it the rest of the way on sheer momentum. But in the whiteout he slowed to a crawl.

Then crept along, feeling through the tires for the road. The children had gone dead silent.

The silence lasted until Ivek lost his feel of the road and knew they had left it. The earth on either side of the Red River had been rolling-pinned by a vast and ancient glacier. The flat fields and prairie were of a time eternal, and the human presence in that expanse was slight. The children knew it and he knew it. They must keep moving or die. Luckily, he'd filled the gasoline tank.

'How about a song?' Ivek shouted.

'What shall we sing?' the Viveky boy called out from a few seats back. His voice trembled. Perhaps he thought that a church hymn would ensure their admittance to heaven.

'We shall sing "Wild Clover."'

Ivek hadn't noticed the girl. She touched her hand to his shoulder. It was Agnid Awbrey, daughter of a Welshman and an Irishwoman, a steady girl of eleven years, whose upbringing proved to be of the finest sort. From her mother, fearless good cheer, and from her father, a soldier who'd fought in Mesopotamia, drinking songs adapted for childish ears. She began. And she taught the other children the words as she went along, just the way Ivek taught his students to learn poems and stirring speeches by heart:

I've been a wild clover all summer long
And I've spent all my money on sunlight and song
But now I am falling asleep under snow
So I can return as wild clover once more.

And it's yes, yea, ever
Yes, yea, ever and more
Shall I be the wild clover
Yea ever and more

The Hollow Children

The song went on, amended verse after verse, with clapping and stamping on the chorus. It roused Ivek's heart and he roared the chorus, too. When the children were tired of that song, there was another, and another:

Fire in our hearts and fire in our minds
Fire in our bodies and souls
Fire, fire, fire, fire!

This one was also accompanied by stamping, pounding, clapping, and roaring. Agnid had probably made it up to keep them warm. But the children eventually quieted, spent.

Ivek kept the school bus moving, sometimes jerking across the prairie and at times gliding on roads, determined not to drive into a ravine or be stopped by any means except that of a warm house or barn. Sometimes his heart sped up so fast that he could hardly breathe. He thought of a child—Mary Wacha, so quiet and so good at math. Or Warwick, the boy who chopped wood for the school stove. Or small-boned Morris, only five years old, whom he'd directed Agnid to bundle in the blanket that usually draped his lap. He would get the children out of his mind only to have their parents crowd in. He knew the parents were praying that the bus had reached the schoolhouse before the worst hit. He thought of his friend John, whose child, the last on his route, he hadn't picked up. Was she wandering in the blizzard? And Agnid's father and mother, and his own wife, her dark hair all in a braid down to her waist. She was at home, and he was glad now that their children had been ill that morning and stayed with her. She would be praying, too. He put her out of his mind and drove on. And on. There was no telling. No telling which direction he was going and he knew not where he was. He knew only that he must not stop.

'The others are hungry,' Agnid said at last. 'I myself have a meat pie so great I cannot eat the whole. Shall I direct us to surrender our lunches and divide the food?'

'Yes.' Ivek spoke without taking his eyes off the nothingness.

'Then I will,' she said, 'and fairly, in spite of the Spiral boys.'

Ivek smiled even in their peril. 'Have they given you trouble?'

'I have them in hand.'

Ivek heard the sounds of negotiation and discussion, voices kept low. He was in a cold sweat because, after hours of flat surface, which he'd thought was possibly the Meridian Road, the bus was bumping over hummocks that didn't feel like snow. For some reason, he imagined that it was a graveyard, although of course that notion was absurd. But then he felt a terrible slickness beneath the wheels. The bus skidded and his heart dropped. He was either farther south or farther west than he'd thought. They hadn't gone down a steep riverbank, so he understood they were on one of the arms of the great deep lake that curved intimately below Tabor. And now, though he knew it was unlikely in the extreme, his blighted mind reviewed the recent stretch of mild days and seized on the vision of the bus plunging to the bottom. He knew that the ice would still be sound throughout the lake, yet his unruly thoughts continued.

Agnid tapped his shoulder and he nearly shrugged her off, but she reached around with the meat pie and let him know the children had agreed he must have it. The instant he bit into the pie, his wheels found purchase. The roads were all straight section roads, though often little more than trails. Reading the way the snow was settling, he renewed his commitment to steering within a few degrees of center, creeping along even more slowly, peering down the edge of his window, which he'd been forced to open a crack. He nosed at the drifts and used a bit of speed to grind through them, always returning to the central line. He went on, on, and on.

The Hollow Children

The wind toyed with the bus, sometimes booming at its sides, sometimes sliding with a low whistle along the window tops. At times, it reached below the hood and shook the engine like a baby's rattle. Ivek would shout to the children, 'Sing that song! Sing that song about the fire!' The children sang for as long as they could. His sweat froze on his forehead. His leg shook as he pressed and let up on the brake. He blinked quickly so he wouldn't run into a tree, few though they were. His mouth was so dry that his tongue was swelling. Staring so desperately hard, he wondered about snow blindness. When the light assumed the flat bluish cast of skim milk, he knew that dusk was upon them, and they fell into the lake.

It wasn't, as he'd imagined, an icy plummet. The water seized them so swiftly that there was no fear or pain, and the fall was surprisingly gradual. They rocked and swayed, lakeweed swirling around their necks and ears. Startled fish swam to the door and by instinct he let them in. He knew they were all lost, forever. He didn't like his thoughts, but he was still glad that his son and daughter were safe at home in the warmth of the good stove. He thought of them burning the wood he'd chopped. There was plenty. But then he heard their voices behind him and realized that they had got on the bus after all.

Sorrow cascaded over him as the bus settled on the bottom of the lake. When there was no use steering any longer, he rose in his grief and turned to the children. He meant to apologize and hoped to recommence the singing, but the children had changed. By unknown means, on the way down to the bottom, the children had become hollow. They were transparent and so frail that they were almost unbearably weighted down by their clothing. Sagging and faint, they listed in the seats, their skin membranous and glistening. Ivek knew that he must not allow them to guess how precarious their existence was, so he went down the center aisle collecting their coats. Once they'd shed their coats, some shot through the windows to the surface, while others would, he realized, spend their days at the bottom, waiting for their families to come to the lake and let down a line they might grasp—

—hold of?

Ivek's eyes were open but somehow they *opened*. He was once again driving on the surface of the blinding earth. He caught a glimpse of the school to the left of the bus before snow slammed shut over the sight. He doubted what he'd seen, but his arms had faith. His hands guided the wheel according to his vision. He sensed that they were in the shadow of something large, a building. He pulled closer to the side. Idled the bus. It was the school. In the lee of the storm, he could see the familiar boards he had painted himself.

He stopped the bus. Opened the door. Wind almost sucked them out. He closed it again and instructed Agnid to sort out her classmates. They lined up in the aisle and made a chain of themselves behind the largest boy, a Spiral, with the smaller children in the middle, and, at the end, Ivek, with Morris grappled to his chest.

The wind wrestled with them as they labored around the side of the school to the door, tumbled in. The children scrambled up and rushed to the stove. Ivek, who always set up the next day's fire before he went home in the evening, unclenched his fingers, clumsily opened the tin matchbox, lighted a cone of newspaper. Fire leaped from the paper, snapped to the splinters of bark. Ivek stood back behind the children, as they crowded close, and the blaze rose up.

Or did it?

The chill in Ivek was far deeper than the fire could touch. The reality of the cold world beneath the ice was stronger than the warmth of the school. He turned away from the stove so the children wouldn't see his tears. What was up and what was down? If he turned back, would the children still be warm and alive? Gritting their teeth in pain and happily whimpering as their numbed feet and fingers prickled to life? Or would they be frail blue human bubbles he'd failed to rescue? Would his son and his daughter be among them? Dissolved to froth? He closed his eyes. Again, he was down there with the fish darting in and out, lakeweed clogging the children's mouths, each seat inhabited by a small, vanished life. And who was he? The driver or the one driven from existence by relentless snow? He reached—

Agnid pressed into his open hand a cup of snow she'd melted. He looked at her. She was sturdy. The water was hot, steeped with a piece of boiled wool she'd cut away from her coat. This was, she said, an old cure that her mother used for wind sickness, times when the mind could no longer bear the wind's moans and mumbles and a person started hearing human voices.

He took the cup, drained it down. It tasted horrible, and he was cured.

Or, rather, he was better. For the drive would leave its mark upon him in a way that someone who had not seen those children, blue and hollow under the lake, would never understand. That was why he wrote it down.

LOVE OF MY DAYS

This happened on the table-flat plains before most farms had telephones. So these incidents came about because news traveled slow. Early one afternoon, Jake Weir went to town to see about a mixture of grains for his horses. When he returned to the farm and went into the house, he saw a stranger sitting at his table.

'What are you doing here?'

Both men said this at the same time.

'This is my house,' said Weir.

'You are mistaken,' said the stranger.

'I must ask you to leave,' said Weir.

'You're the one who should leave.'

'I guess I'll have to go back to town and get the sheriff.'

'Go get him then. I don't care.'

The man stood up. He wasn't large or threatening, old or young, red-haired or dark-haired or blond. Everything about him was middling. Weir was confused by the man's unusual conviction, though. He half believed the man did own the place, although he himself had bought it the previous year. Yet maybe there was some odd reason that the man had a claim. Weir got back into his good black buggy and turned around. So responsive were his two horses that he barely needed to shift his grip on the reins. He made good time and easily located the sheriff, who was sitting at the courthouse in the presence of a judge. Weir explained the predicament, found he was in the right, and proceeded to obtain a warrant for eviction. Sheriff Flower and Deputy Otto Klocke drove out to Weir's farmstead, with Weir following along in his buggy. By then a thin wet snow was coming down.

As they came into the yard, the front door of the house gaped open, but when the horses stopped the door swung shut. The men climbed down off their rigs, and Sheriff Flower approached the house.

'May I come in and dry my feet?' he asked.

'There's no place in here to dry your feet' was the reply.

'Well, then,' said Flower, 'I want to feed my team.'

'Go to the stable and feed your team. I don't care.'

Both men listened hard on either side of the door.

'I know who you are,' said the voice from inside, at last. 'You're Flower, the sheriff.'

'Well, who are you?' Flower asked.

Something in the sheriff's tone deeply aggravated and frightened the man behind the door.

'I am John Timble.' The voice wavered, then gathered. 'I am above the state. I am a detective. A Pinkerton.'

'All right, John. Come out,' said Flower. He lifted his revolver and stepped warily off the porch.

Out John came with his rifle on his hip. He pulled the trigger, then dropped the gun as if in alarm. The sheriff's death was swift but not instantaneous. He still had time to fire. Later on, it was found that Flower's bullet had struck Timble's hand, which would have thrown off the murderer's aim if Timble hadn't fired in that deadly instant in which one man has desperate certainty and owns surprise. The shot startled Weir's team of horses and they veered in unison toward the barn. Attempting to vault onto the driving seat, Weir went head first into the buggy box so that his legs were pumping in the air. The man who thought he was above the state retrieved the rifle and fired shots at Weir's legs, sending bullets through his overshoe and cuffs. The buggy stopped before a fence. Up came John Timble.

'Get out. I just want the team.'

The murderer jumped onto the seat, taking up the reins as he covered Weir with the rifle. Weir pushed himself out of the buggy and stepped away, looking not at the rifle but at his two horses. Timble drove around the yard once, and Weir watched the killer closely as he made off with the horses. At least the man knew what he was doing. Weir and Klocke ran to help Sheriff Flower but found that there was no life in him.

'What are we to do now?' said Klocke.

'You're the deputy,' said Weir.

He went into the house and took the quilt off his bed. The two men carried Flower to the sheriff's wagon, his body sagging dreadfully between them. They hoisted him into the wagon bed, and Weir covered him with the quilt. The men tried to hurry to town and sound the alarm, but Flower's spooked and jangled horses seesawed and balked. The left horse just wanted to shamble along, while the right horse pulled with frantic jerks. They weren't even the same size.

Weir was in back with the body. His teeth rattled and he felt as if his head was going to burst. He kept tucking the quilt down over Flower's face. He did this tenderly. He'd stood with Flower a few years before when a certain town element had tried to oust him, and now Flower had given his life in an encounter that seemed pointless and altogether Weir's fault. He might have done a better job than Klocke with the driving, but he couldn't leave Flower. It took them nearly two hours to travel seven miles, and a bit more time for Klocke to get straight the wording of the alert.

John Timble has killed Sheriff Flower and is running fugitive. Take him alive or dead. He is known to be armed with'—here Klocke consulted Weir, whose weapon in Timble's hands had killed the sheriff—*'a .38 caliber Winchester.'*

'He has plenty of ammunition,' Weir added, thinking of recent purchases he'd left in the kitchen, heat coming to his face, 'and the fastest driving team in the whole damn county.'

His team consisted of the best possible combination—a mare and her foal, now a four-year-old gelding. He'd got the mare at auction for a song, no, a short tune. No one had known what she was. But Weir had seen it. Quarter horse, mustang, and possibly Morgan. Dark and wonderful. The four-year-old had a black line down his back. The mare was persnickety sometimes, but her offspring always steadied her. They ran in balance and paced themselves to any deficiency in the other's mood. He'd trained them up until their gaits were matched so perfectly that sometimes he had trouble breathing for the joy.

Weir was sick about the sheriff, no question, but now the undertaker had him and there was nothing to be done. He turned his attention to what had happened and was glad the murderer, who'd been wearing Weir's best hat, blue shirt, and his other jacket, hadn't killed him, too. However, he was beginning to regret not putting up a struggle when the man took the reins into his hands. He kept thinking back to how Timble had circled the yard before pulling onto the road. The murderer had a light and certain touch with the horses and drove pretty well, considering he'd just ended a sheriff's life.

SCORES OF MEN posse'd up when they got the alert. Some on horses, some in wagons. Some marched back and forth in front of their houses and farms. It was a cold December afternoon, and it would be a cold night for those patrolling the roads and crossings. But a warm night for John Timble.

Ten days after H. W. Cherian moved his family onto a farmstead south of Tabor, he heard someone drive into the yard. H. W. had been putting in order his request for a bank loan, while his wife, Karlet, finished up a bit of midnight baking. Holding a kerosene lamp, he opened the kitchen door and spoke to a well-mannered man who had become lost in his quest to find a nearby farm. The man stepped down from the buggy with a pleasant gesture.

'I can sleep with my team in the barn if you'd give us shelter and a little food,' said the man. 'John Timble.' He held out his hand for a shake. 'My hope is that we might be neighbors.' H. W. did not recognize the farm the man said he was looking for but explained that he'd been there only a short while.

'Luck upon you,' said Timble.

Cherian thanked him.

'A man can make a lot of money,' Timble observed.

'Looks like you did pretty well for yourself,' said H. W., shining the lamp on the good buggy and handsome team.

'So I have,' said Timble.

Together, they stabled the horses. Timble pressed money on his host for hay, and also grain, some of which he'd take along come morning. From the barn, they walked into the house. Timble nodded to Karlet. She noted that his hat and jacket were good but his trousers and shoes were worn out. She recognized the farm he'd spoken of as the one her family had once owned, belonging now to someone named Weir.

'Torn on a rough board,' said Timble, opening his palm.

Karlet went to her cupboard and found a clean rag to use as a bandage and a tot of whiskey to give the man and to wash out the injury. She knew who the man was, knew a bullet furrow when she saw one. The house had no phone; whatever trouble there was she could ignore for now. So she gave him the last of the chicken. It was a thick piece of chicken, tender and well cooked, sandwiched between two generously buttered slices of hot bread. That night

John Timble slept well, on the hard kitchen floor, with a throbbing hand and the rifle beneath his blanket, but also with a warm place in his belly and the scent of still cooling bread around him. The next morning, he helped H. W. care for his stock and accepted Karlet's invitation to stay for breakfast with the family.

'I know how you like your eggs cooked,' she told Timble.

The two children were setting plates down on the table. At their mother's words they spun toward her. They didn't care how she could already know how their guest might like his eggs. Their eyes were only mute with disappointment that he had been offered the eggs. Timble cast his gaze down, hid his smile.

'I don't need an egg,' he said.

He'd found out while helping with the chores that a slaughtering weasel had got into the henhouse through a crack. In the heat of its bloodlust, the weasel had killed the entire flock. The hens now existed in jars packed and canned on a cellar shelf. Soup from the carcass of the one chicken that the family had spared itself bubbled on the stove, he could smell it, but eggs were few anyway in December and eggs there would be no more.

I will eat an egg soon enough, thought Timble.

Now the scent and sizzle of salt pork filled the house and soon large pieces of bread fried in the fat appeared. There was also porridge and strong hot coffee. Timble thought of the blood that had bloomed on the sheriff's chest and he asked for another cup. He drank that down.

'I must leave now,' he said.

He put coins from his inner vest into the children's hands, then picked up the rifle. I was cornered but I am no killer, he thought, as he and the farmer new to the area walked out. The problem now was he'd got himself too far to the south, instead of heading west toward the coteau. The problem also was there'd been new snow and he was easy to track. The problem for a while was he kept losing his grip on his thoughts. He'd worked on these very farms when they had belonged to other men. He'd worked any job he could find and secured wealth for the landowners. After felling trees in northern Wisconsin, he had suddenly hopped a train back to this valley, where he'd spent the ardor of his youth. His ideas were jumbled. He'd slept cold in camps near the railroad with the hobos and the yeggers until he'd become a yegger, too. After he'd arrived in the valley, he had found himself walking to the first place he knew, and then the next and the next in this limitless place. He hoped that the sheriff, whom he'd noticed buying licorice drops just the other day, wasn't mortally hurt.

The men took care with the buggy. As H. W. Cherian stroked the mare, he noticed the new tack.

'These horses are sheer gorgeous,' he said.

They stood back to admire their rich depth of brown. Had Cherian lived there even a few more weeks he would have known who had reared and trained the team. Timble nodded his thanks, gathered up the reins, and swept his finger from his forehead to say goodbye. And all the while he and Cherian, still warm from their breakfast, were being watched by two very cold men.

WEIR AND HIS friend Hartig were hiding a couple of hundred yards beyond the farmstead. They had been out all night tracking the murderer. Just an hour ago, Weir had recognized the tracks of his own buggy wheels and the shoes on his horses. From a stand of trees on the east edge of the farm, they were waiting to get the jump on Timble. Weir had watched the killer lead his horses to the buggy. To his satisfaction and relief, he saw Timble harness the team back in the same position as the day before. By this he knew the man didn't want to monkey with the setup. That was the satisfaction. The relief was because the gelding's distinction was a paddle foot. In the wrong position, he might have cut his mother's foreleg in a wild chase, should such an awful situation come about. Weir prayed it would not. He breathed fervently, trying to calm himself. He and Hartig were armed only with revolvers. They both meant to stop Timble as he passed them, if he set out east. To their intense disappointment, Timble headed west.

The two men rolled into the farmyard and told the family about the killed sheriff and the stolen team. H. W. was aghast, stood outside slapping his arms as the men drove off after Timble. As Karlet well knew, a bullet had made a deep groove in the outlaw's palm. His was a hand thickened by labor, but his control of the horses and even his aim would still be spoiled. She went back to her wash. Even after it was all over, she didn't tell anyone what she knew, especially not her husband, who'd failed to repair the henhouse when they had moved in. She didn't tell her children, either, but she did tell her grandchildren. They asked her to tell them many times, in fact, about the murderer who'd worked on her father's farm and who, the next time she saw him, ate the last of the weasel-killed chicken in a sandwich. She told how, the next morning, he had refused the eggs and given the children, who became their parents, coins. Karlet knew how he'd earned the coins or used to earn them—he had kept stock, pitched hay, plowed, managed the threshing teams, dug a well that had collapsed and nearly killed him. It had seemed from his matched horses and nice shirt that he'd come up in the world, and she was sorry that was not true.

WHY DID I say that I was a Pinkerton man? Timble asked himself this question when he noticed the wagon following. Why did I say that I was above the state? Those words had sounded fine and strong but they had belonged to a different man. A man who would take offense at the sheriff's reedy voice. No more than that. Timble's dry fury had grabbed him like a hungry spirit. In fact, he had been very hungry at the time. Now he was well fed. The wagon behind him dropped away. The road flowed along like milk pouring from a jug. He forgot what he had done. The packed snow was hard and clean, lightly dusted over. The sun was brilliant and mild on the western hills, where hardly anyone lived except Sioux Indians. Timble started thinking that he didn't want to creep up on Indians. Eventually, he turned around. He started back toward the men who were hunting him.

Along the road he found a stock tank where the ice had been broken and water gleamed. He stopped there, watered the horses judiciously, and gave them a little grain, stroking the crest of one, then the other, as they ate from the bottom of a crumpled sack. Starting out again, he walked them, but not so they'd cool down too much. Then he asked them again for their effortless fast trot. He could feel their enjoyment along the reins.

Every town and most farms along the way now had the alert. Farmers were up their windmills and atop their barns and in other spots of vantage, scouting for Timble. Men were out with every variety of weapon. They were swarming along the border between Wakazonta and White Rock. A man named Budack stopped the wagon Weir was driving and threw his carbine rifle to Hartig.

'Let's keep our heads,' said Weir, alarmed. 'Don't go blasting away around my horses.'

'Don't worry,' said Hartig.

'Let me take your place,' said Budack to Weir.

'No.'

Budack reached up with his powerful skinny arms, grabbed Weir's jacket, and wrenched him off the seat. Hartig snatched up the reins, putting down the rifle. Then Budack vaulted on in Weir's place, yelling, 'Git! Git!' He picked up the whip and used it, so that Hartig was hard put to steady the wagon. Budack picked up the rifle. He had seen Timble driving toward the crossing just ahead. The horses jumped forward. Weir ran behind the wagon. From a distance, he saw his buggy and horses with Timble driving make the crossing, and heard the shooting start.

MUST BE THAT I killed Flower, thought Timble. Now he was traveling along the snow-blown fields, past little outcrops and section roads. Again he left behind the wagon that was after him and enjoyed the flow of peace along the reins. There'd never been anything like this before in his life and he didn't want it to end. Therefore, he hadn't stopped when he saw men along the road trying to flag him down. He'd just sailed through the crossing and over the frozen sloughs beyond. He hadn't thought why, but as soon as the wagons drew near again, he knew. Hanging was not for a man such as himself. He was meant to drive marvelous creatures. And not yet had he asked of them the utmost! Once the shooting started up, however, he slapped the reins down lightly and thrilled to the heat of power in his hands. The horses were flying like hawks and he knew this country well, having worked these farms; if he could shake his pursuers again, he wanted to visit the rolling country and small rivers just east of White Rock. He wanted to see the tall winter jackrabbits bouncing across the snows. The road faltered, and he let the horses pick their way along. He'd make up the distance, he believed, and if cornered again he still had time to kill himself.

BUDACK DID THE shooting and used his cavalry rifle. He'd been seventeen years old serving during the last of the Indian Wars. He considered himself afraid of nothing, though to tell the truth he'd only guarded starving stragglers and left when the buffalo soldiers turned everything upside down. When they relieved his company down in Sisseton he'd quit. Since that time, decades had passed and he'd tried everything he could think of to get a job as sheriff or deputy sheriff or any kind of official in any town at all, but people turned away—as if there were something about him.

It was not until he threw down Weir and leaped up beside Hartig that he got his chance. He would do anything to bring down a criminal. He was furious that they'd let the man skim by. It nearly maddened him. He tried to hang on and kept shooting, reloading, shooting, whether or not he was in range. Hartig side-eyed him and told him to settle. There was rough road ahead, and they gained ground on the buggy. At one point, up ahead, Weir's horses had to turn nearly sideways on the broken path. Budack had the rifle on his shoulder in that moment. He took the shot. And to bring down his man he aimed for the horse.

Why haven't they managed to shoot me yet? Timble puzzled as he went off on foot, walked and ran, stopping occasionally to try to kill the man who had jumped down to pursue him. Budack was an eager devil. He'd even fired a bullet that grazed Timble's scalp and knocked him down for a moment. Timble entered the big White Rock ravine with plenty of ammunition. The trees were glowing with hoarfrost down there, picked out golden by the low rays of sunlight. He'd got hauled out of caved earth once and went from dead to living. The years since had been gravy. Oh, it was good to be above ground. Today was like one of those dances he'd been at from time to time, where, just when you mean to leave, the music and the lights pick up. But you can't stay. Someone is waiting, he thought. I know what I had. Milk pouring from a jug. I will never have the like of that drive again. I know these farms. Ate well in my life. I've no complaint except for want of land. Yet, that bread! And also, yet.

Who would take such an evil shot? Horses pull for each other and he could see the one on the left was bred from the one on the right and they'd no call to shoot a son's mother.

A soundless drench of colors smote Timble.

ONCE THE TACK and harness was untangled, the son lifted himself away from his mother. He stood alone as he was being rubbed dry with hay. When half of you is gone, the half left behind begins its long descent into a cold strange barn. No matter how warm you get you are never warm and no matter how much you eat you are never full. You are out of harness but somehow pulling the entire weight. At least the authority came to him. Cradled his jaw, kept running the brush along his back, made the sounds they make when they must stand up to a loss. It wasn't enough, but the man stayed near and made noises *why if only and why and if only and if only why*—all sorts of nonsense—and gave shape to the suffering.

AFTER THE COLORS cleared away, Timble was surprised to see Beatril walking toward him over the snow. She was wearing her summer dress of rose pink with tiny checks; her sleeves were rolled up over her strong tanned forearms and she was wiping her hands on her apron, as if she'd just washed them. She was walking quickly, purposefully, but not running, so he didn't think that he'd been hit very badly. Her brown hair was loose, as if she had just washed that, too. Her hair was blowing about her shoulders and as she got near to him she smiled.

'I seen your sister this very morning,' he said to her.

As if this were an ordinary meeting, she made an exasperated face that was nonetheless full of love. Her fractious sister, Karlet, had been a favorite of their conversation. Each of the daughters had a name that began with the letters of the name their father had chosen, upended by the letters that their mother had insisted upon. Beatril was the oldest, then Nantiv, and at last Karlet. The farm had failed three years in a row, and they had moved to town, renting out the house and land, leaving Timble to hunt down jobs and hop trains to follow the harvest. He'd got stuck in Nebraska. Upon his return, he found that Beatril had contracted typhus and died of it. He'd walked back to the train and kept moving—east, west, and, of course, south down the harvest corridor. How the years passed. The things he'd seen and done. But he remembered best the year he and Beatril found that she was for him and he was for her. (He'd remembered everything, times over, bucking along in boxcars.) How they'd shared a jug of ginger water in the heat of the day, how she shook off her apron and laid out a picnic of bread and apples. Before he left, they lay down in the brittle yellow grass and watched grasshoppers spring from tip to tip above their heads. In the peace of early twilight they had turned to each other.

'Love of my days.'

He had said it to her then and he said it to her now. Someone's boots squeaked on the snow. Budack loomed over them, his revolver out. Kneeling beside Timble, Beatril grasped his hand and said, 'Don't mind him.'

DOMAIN

Seven corporations control the afterlife, and many people spend their lives amassing the money to upload into the best. Others, like me, assume they will need a scholarship and pile up experience. I piled up one too many. Shortly after my fall, I applied to Asphodel. I knew of course that this particular domain, or afterlife provider, was run by the oldest entity in the business. Asphodel was known to have one of the most secure and complete visual terrains. Artists always chose Asphodel if they could afford it, and I was an artist before my accident. I knew some parents who'd had to download a child under grievous circumstances, and they had chosen Asphodel for the schools and the reliable surrogacy. For one other specific reason, too, Asphodel was most attractive to me. As a consequence, that first morning I was so nervous about the interview process that I refused pain medication. I wanted to be mentally sharp. As I was wheeled along the corridor, past the swooping black characters glazed into the hospital tiles, I thought I might have made a mistake. The pain was that distracting. But as soon as the questions began, I regained my concentration.

The interviewer was a square red cube sitting in the middle of the room on a stainless-steel table.

Your name?

Bernadette.

Named for the saint?

Yes.

Any other associations?

My mother was a Catholic and a theologian. She was chosen by the Church and completely subsidized, her understanding was that valuable. Since she was uploaded, gratis, we have communicated every day. But I chose Asphodel because I do not share her system of symbols. I was not raised in the formality of her religion and find comfort in literature.

I smoothly volunteered that my father had chosen a premature upload before they were outlawed, and that his decision had been secured since then. I gave his name and effortlessly moved on. The cube did not react. My practice had paid off.

Do you mind if we scan?

No.

I closed my eyes, dizzy, and requested additional oxygen. As deliberately as I could, using the training my mother had insisted on since I was young, I called up a series of images. These began when I was about five years old. They were detailed, visual, aural, descriptive, emotional, as concrete as I could possibly manage. I remembered the wooden front steps of our house, the paint worn off the risers to show gray wood. The temperature of the wood in every season. The green of Virginia creeper, the leaves fluttering off the porch in summer wind, stiff with morning dew, half wilted in full sun. The tiny knuckles of the vines clutching the wire of the screens. The lobes of lilacs. The scent. The sour green balls of new grapes and the heavy, peeling brown loops of grapevines. And from the front steps, the horizon and the sky. My mother had coached me to memorize the sky every morning and evening. I used the sky as my masking image—you could not get through it to the bad thing that had happened. The sky was my protection. I could pass through years of sky, a slideshow of sky, endless mental snapshots. A thousand skies and a thousand more. I went through them at a leisurely pace, skipping no small detail. The sky had always been my favorite mental exercise, and one that, I now hoped, would increase my value for Asphodel.

Impressive.

The interviewer changed to a thoughtful maroon red and quit the scan.

You were coached?

By my mother.

Memory games as a child?

Yes.

The pain was becoming difficult to ignore. It was taking some attention.

An unusually pure visual memory. The best I have encountered. Your mother did her job well.

She knew that the chances were slim that we would ever have the means to afford Asphodel.

The interviewer agreed, a quiet yellow tinge.

And then, this.

Yes.

Can you describe the accident?

I was climbing. I climb buildings.

Free-climbing. It is . . . not exactly illegal.

No. But I was trespassing.

A small matter. We will not take that into consideration.

I was climbing the Guthrie Theater here in Minneapolis, where my father's play was performed this year.

Yes, we know about your father.

The pain was overwhelming. I began to breathe deeply, explosively, but could not help crying out.

What is it?

My legs, you know, everything.

Yes, said the interviewer, you're broken. But you have a good chance for some limited capacity, enough to survive. You could have a life. A life here. Are you sure you want to . . .

Yes, yes, as soon as possible. Now.

So they came with the drugs and scheduled the download for tomorrow.

Neural Cascade

You say goodbye to your body very carefully. The toenails you've clipped and polished, the vulnerable instep, the ankles and shins you've barked, the sometimes unreliable knees, the calves you've shared, thighs your lover has grazed his hand along and inside, goodbye to the dark of you, the brilliant unshattering or raveling that seemed at one time the way your spirit also traveled, outward, everywhere, beginning from the heated core. Goodbye to gut that pinched with hunger or split with gas, goodbye to asshole and nervous sphincter that permitted a loud fart when you laughed in a movie on your first date. Goodbye to vagina, wait, goodbye again to black, brown, purple, gold, mauve, red, bleeding leaves of skin, vulva, and stubborn fickle clitoris that maddened with indifference or was whiplash sensitive—goodbye. Goodbye old uterus, old love, old capacious fist, and goodbye outraged liver. Goodbye sweet lungs with your faint bubbling black carcinogenic lace and your amazed resilience and heart, dearest heart. So long pumps. Goodbye throat-licked and suave collarbone in a low-cut black sheath, and arms that held and clung to other arms and other edifices, arms and legs that climbed and back I never really saw. Breasts always in the way. Nipples. Hands, oh my hands, piano-player hands. Hands that grasped and pulled and slapped and touched so tenderly beyond my appetite. Hands of my appetite, goodbye. Ears, neck, earlobes, and mouth of a million golden tastes and mouth that knew food of every type and tastes of all description but above all things mouth, goodbye, and goodbye tongue, that loved the kisses and also the body of my husband. I do not have to say goodbye to my eyes. I'll still see. And in fact I will feel the feelings of all parts of my body. I will feel the eidetic past. But the broken body I am leaving behind will be recycled for parts and then sold for remaining mineral content. Even the physical brain, soon transferred, neural file by file, molecule by molecule, into the liqui-chip. A dumb lump of fat will remain.

***

The holes will be drilled tomorrow. The liquid memory slowly introduced to the still living brain. The software drug binds and copies as it eats the living memory. The drug contains a disciplined nucleocytovirus that takes instructions and is formulated to mimic and store consciousness—here is the beauty, the complexity—store the individual consciousness in a form that can be siphoned from the brain when loading is complete and then absorbed by Charon. She, the program, is the reader of my life text who will transfer me into the field.

***

Last night, before I went to sleep, I had the nurse access my mother and push the screen up close to my face so that we could talk. She had chosen to be old and reassuring, lined and pallid, with a sweetness in her face I can remember only rarely in earthly life. We talked and talked.

Mama, what will it feel like? Will it hurt?

You'll be all right.

All right like in childbirth? All right after I'm ripped apart?

Her face slackened. She didn't want to say. But she loves me, and she did.

The virus cannot accomplish its task without your full alertness. You'll feel it all. Old emotions. Every pain and pleasure. Every fuckup and every fear. A deluge. You will believe you are going mad. (They do not read you because they do not find readings during the process reliable, so don't worry, they won't see anything.) Still, it is a drowning. Some don't surface, it is true. But you will come back, I promise. Remember, I made you strong. What helps is to find an image. Something to hold on to.

We stared at each other for a long time. Her face kept flickering through the many ages and personae she'd assumed. Her face would not be the image I'd hold on to. I needed something more solid.

Pick him, she said, suddenly, softly.

I thought at first she meant my husband, or my son, though his image is inaccessible. But she didn't. And now I saw it in her face.

I know why you're choosing his domain.

Her voice trembled, a whisper.

And she was right. The one uncontaminated truth. My father, my changeless hatred. I'd hold on to him.

***

Fasten your seat belt, it's going to be a bumpy ride.

Are you kidding?

I'm not good with reassurance, said the technician. But you're lucky. You're going to a top-notch place.

Domain

They put me in a flexangle, a hard gel that closes around you up to the chin. When I was immobilized, the woman picked up the drill.

You're going to feel this. Everybody feels it. Try thinking past it.

The technician paused.

While you can still think.

***

They try to introduce the liquid as slowly and gently as possible, but at a certain point it saturates. By then the virus is moving quickly, humming along, sparking and devouring, capturing, destroying. From the first instant, I know that I cannot endure it for another instant, even to gain eternal life. And then I do endure it. I go on. I have his face in focus for a moment, here and there, but then he changes and I just hold on to the hate.

I whip around it like a pole. I fly off it like a flag. That hatred, planted in calcareous shit, gets me through the first part. But then it wilts and at the base of it is love.

Asphodel

They let my body stay where it was for the hours it took the system to read me, and then for me to focus my new eyes. The results are better when you get to see the technicians put away your old carcass, apparently, because I saw them do me. Oh, they were respectful enough, took the tubes out without yanking. But I could see well enough to tell my body had stiffened a bit, already, and I'd shat myself all the way up my back straight out of my diaper.

Well, never again.

I have a new body now and it's made of thought.

Louise Erdrich

***

When I arrived in Asphodel, I was placed in the transition program, a cross between purgatory and a hospital, a quiet, calm place where my task was to understand the entity that I would now be, forever. Here, the siphoners come to pick and choose what they want to add to their domain. Using human memory, they are building a complex and ordered world that replicates and outdoes the first one, into which we are all born. Asphodel is the deepest and most thoroughly finished, but there are still gaps in its reality, places, even in the transition program, where the tiles quit or go rubbery when they are actually ceramic or where the windows contain the wrong light for the hour of the day. But the personnel are fully integrated and know not to change too drastically while you are looking at them, which is something I cannot do when I first arrive.

Remember, your appearance reflects your every mood, thought, emotion, says a silky woman. Her hand is on my arm. She has given her hand just the right amount of warmth and my own memory of skin blooms in response.

Master it, master it, she croons. Yes, yes, you may take a deep breath. The nanoneuralcircuitry that is now you will remember what it was to take a deep breath and your brain, or the superfile of your brain, will remember it too. Take a deep breath. Your fear is purple. Your appearance.

I'm a cloud, I say, looking down at my legs. Insubstantial as a cloud. And I'm still in pain. The fuck! I'm still in pain!

Wait, she says, calm yourself and take a deep breath.

I do. The pain is gone.

And remember how your legs feel. Your workout two days before your fall.

Yes.

Domain

I look down. My legs are perfect. I am naked.

What were you wearing?

What the hell? Maybe I was wearing a low-necked black cocktail dress.

Now you're cooking! Her voice is delighted. I smell egg, onions, mushrooms frying in butter, and my mouth waters.

I think I'm hungry.

Yes, you're hungry. And you're going to eat. And if you concentrate fully on what you are eating, it will be the best thing you've ever tasted.

***

So how to find him. How to kill him. How to savagely or subtly murder my father in a world where there isn't any death?

***

I look into the mirrored wall and my face is fecal, feral, frantic, fraught, festering. No façade.

I work then for months (the sun comes up here, the sun goes down) on my physical control. Then one day I ask how we travel to other places. Everyone begins in the place they used to live. I am in Minneapolis and have my apartment. But my cache of skies and any other useful memories have been added, painstakingly, to the deeply convincing fabric of this world.

We have a marvelous transportation system, says my guide. Very real. You can book flights almost anywhere now, take trains, whatever you want. Or you can scroll.

Can you teach me to do that?

Nobody can teach it.

How does it work? What happens?

Intense lucid dreaming. You teach yourself to dream yourself wherever you want to be. You have to learn how to stay conscious in your dream, but not to wake up. You don't want to drop yourself.

And people? Can I look someone up from my past?

Of course, once you've got the hang of it. But it will be hard to tell whether you're accessing the actual person or just your memory of the person.

I feel funny asking this, I say, but something occurred to me.

Ask anyway.

Is there any way out of here? Do people exit? Leave? Are they ever expelled?

She turns bright pink. An orange bubble bursts from her lips. She laughs in surprise.

No, she says, of course not, that never happens, except . . .

Her eyes go black. Her face and arms fade into the wall. I can see through her. It is as though she's made of tissue and her voice is faint.

It is rare. Yet people have been erased by other people here, she says. Then she readjusts. She's solid and rosy.

What does it take to do something like that?

Shock, she says, her voice a whisper. There was an assassin sent many years ago, I heard, from the fore-life. He caught the victim completely unaware. The guy was stunned, paralyzed, and he just . . . she laughs. There is no other word for . . . deleted himself?

The Library

My father has become the library. He will be dangerous to enter. In his time, he was a leading playwright and scholar. But his childhood memories of the library were most interesting to Asphodel, and he has been hard at work constructing this new library ever since he entered.

Domain

His childhood library still exists in the small town where he grew up, a sweet old county library made of red sandstone with brass handles on the doors and a broad oak desk, stained dark, where the books are checked out and returned. He remembered every inch of it, and more, he remembered every library he had studied in as a young man, and older, as he became the kind of person who used libraries exclusively and bought real books of the old kind, made of paper and print and glue. He knew the smell of them and the weight of them and the texture of their covers. What books he didn't know he could imagine in convincing detail. Every book in the fore-life has long been auto-scanned into our universe and so it only takes the proper thought, an operational thought, to fill those tangible but empty ciphers of books with words. This, then, is my father's work. The library is his mind. He is filling it with an infinite number of books in which he can play, hide, or be part of whatever chapter or incident he chooses.

***

To murder my father in that library may be impossible, but it must be done. I have to surprise him to death. Make him completely vulnerable and open. His mind must be utterly relaxed so that when I strike he cannot deflect the blow. And the blow must be true and final. He cannot be erased by increments, but just like that. One blow. One instant. He must reverse. Blow up. Disintegrate. Delete.

Inevitable

Of course it comes back, in the night when all the monitors are off and I am a shifting flame that does not burn. That is the other attraction of Asphodel. The contract stipulates night privacy. No dream siphoning. A freedom resembling the real earth freedom to retain an unknowable existence, an unconsciousness that cannot be tapped. Asphodel's cheaper sister, the Meadows, mines dreams. There are many who do not care or never notice this intrusion, but I would. I love my sleep now, my nothingness, my unnecessary dream life. I would not technically have to sleep at all in Asphodel, but I chose sleep, as do most people (though not my father, it is reported). I love sleep because now that I am immortal it is my only way to experience relief from consciousness.

I also love sleep because my son comes back to me. He visits often now in dreams. His image has become accessible. He was six years old, the tenderest age, a mop of fine, heavy red hair like his father's (mine is black, short, coarse, when I am in default appearance). I used to put my cheek to his hair when he came in flushed from playing outside and I breathed in the avid October cold of cold boy. He was always moving, quitless, bumbling, and exuberant. When sad, he was cast down, inconsolable. He died in the care of my father and my father let him go, did not make the essential call that would have allowed him, my son, to be with me now. My father waited until it was too late to salvage him. He did this because of his religious certainty.

My father's plays were about the need for death, the unthought consequences of immortality. The moral human was the human with the courage to really die and stay dead. But ten years after the real death of my son, my father chose, as I've said, to voluntarily end his physical life and enter Asphodel. He was in perfect health. He had simply changed his mind. He considered his talents, his genius, his knowledge, too valuable to risk the loss. It was a considered leap which for years he had persuaded many to resist.

Some Travel

To leave the vicinity of my father and perfect my skills, I travel. I can scroll now. I am in Barcelona of 1998 on the Ramblas, the great strolling avenue leading to the sea. Composed of combined memory, people appear and disappear much the way they always did, crowds passing, mimes in exquisite costumes poised until a coin is dropped before them. One, a dark lady in a magnificent gray gown, wearing gray face paint, black hair, black flowers, appears to be sleeping, head slightly cocked. Her crown is a black serpent coiled and poised to strike above her brow. I drop my money into an ornate urn and her eyes open slowly, great black pooling eyes. She reaches incrementally for my hand and kisses my fingers, caresses my wrist, in languid slow motion lets my fingers go, and drifts back into her slumber. The snake is real. Its tongue flickers, scarlet, curious.

I know that some uploaded tourist from another age remembered her in great detail and placed her here, but with a live snake, artful. Others have remembered the Gaudí buildings and Park Güell, Alexander Calder's Mercury Fountain and the desperate sellers of roses—refugees who haunted the restaurants with ravaged eyes. When I buy a rose from one man, he says, *Remember me*, and I know that in someone else's life on real earth this man said the same thing and his bleak eyes were fixed in someone's consciousness, so that although he has surely not acquired the means to enter an afterlife himself and has died the real death with billions of other humans, this rose seller will live in this particular corporation's version of the city of Barcelona, whispering, forever, *Remember me*.

Waking

I used to love taking naps on early spring afternoons before the leaves had budded out, when the air was bright and cool. I would lie on my back with my aching legs on a pillow and pull over me a down comforter, a gift from my mother. Awakening, I would allow my consciousness to drift back into my body. There would always be, first, the sword of grief, which I would allow to stake me to the mattress, but then as my waking awareness increased and I felt where my flesh ended and the soft bedclothes and pillows began, a soft shudder of ecstasy filled me and with each breath increased and subsided, subsided and increased, until at last I opened my eyes. I do this now, whenever I wake, only now I do this for what may be hours, or days, for time on this side of things is not sidereal and relentless. Time is gentle. We are flowers. Opening and closing as we respond to the temperature and the light of our thoughts. And when I do assume my body and my awareness, and when I do decide where to go, what I would like to do, my actions add to the texture of this world, so that everything I do here has a purpose. The layering of consciousness upon consciousness makes, for instance, a beautiful park steadier, more palpable, more enjoyable to others. This is a thing we unknowingly did, perhaps, on the other side, but it is so important here that we all have work; every moment of our existence is creation for others to enjoy, an occupation that was once called art; we are all artists on this side.

When I murder my father, that moment will create a rip in the fabric of time. Like art, it will jar the past, pierce the future.

The Card

In order to use the library, you must apply for a card. The program set up to process the request is tall and pleasant. She is neither young nor old, and gazes at me over the oak counter with its dull green blotter. She wears small wire-rimmed glasses. Her hair is brown, streaked with gray, rolled back in a chignon. She wears a dress of brown and white checks. In a low voice, she requests my identification, and then bends over slightly to copy my name onto a blue library card. I have

Domain

used my mother's name most of my adult life, and it is a common surname. The librarian returns my identification. I am hoping my introduction into the system will be unremarked. I watch the program write my name in lovely, old-fashioned D'Nealian script and I wonder if the pleasant librarian is my father. He can take any form in the library; however, this processing of cards is painstaking and a little silly. Beneath him, I would think. A waste of his time, which although infinite is still *his*. The blue piece of cardboard is handed to me, a rectangle with rounded edges. I will have to present this card each time I take out a book, a detail meant to be charming. The librarian is changing the date in her rubber stamp and re-inking the felt pad in its metal case as I leave. My father has made each detail— astounding work. I want so badly to examine the books. I am so curious about the editions, the design, the paper, the typefaces, all that he has added to the veracity of his world. But I continue on out the door, down the broad stone steps, because I do not want to come across him accidentally. Even though I have chosen an entirely different form today, I do not want *him* to surprise *me*.

The Brick

*I practice my disguise. I will be his mother, to whom he was deeply at-*tached. My grandmother, a woman vivid in my memory, a woman lost to real death, as was her belief. She was deerlike and gentle and softly silent. I call her up, I conjure her, I become her. An olive-green dress. Sweet brown eyes, whitely faded hair. And then in an instant I shift and become myself. I have a weapon, of course, to compound the shock and throw my father into the reflex cascade that will end him. It will be the same object that ended my son's life. A falling brick from a church renovation tumbling unknown off a workman's scaffold. My father carried Edan to the side of the churchyard and sat on the bench with him, watched as he died, and at last called me up to say, weeping, He is gone. Instead of calling Asphodel or some other company's rescue team, all one-digit numbers that can be dialed into the human wrist, he allowed my son to go.

I will be my father's mother. Then all of a sudden, myself, with a brick in my hand which I will smash down upon his head. My advantage will be the powerfully violent imagery which I will add to the constructed reality—his terror, blood, reeling fall, death, every second of which I rehearse until it feels that it has already happened. It hasn't happened, no, I reassure myself. Yet it has already begun.

All Things Are Made of Consciousness

You'd think the weather would always be nice, the sun would shine all the time, dogs would not bite nor flowers wilt nor impatient people shove. You'd think there would be no lines to stand in. No rotten eggs, spoiled milk. The redolent odor of skunk in spring. Shoes that pinch. Warped wooden doors that do not completely shut. You'd think that here it would be perfect.

But it is better than perfect. It is beyond everything I could have imagined or can now convey. The twists and turns and quirks and elegance of mind make it so. The strangeness, the humor, the mistakes. The great elm outside my window is the tree another person had memorized and rethought. Each sawtooth leaf and ragged twig, each whorl of thick, gray bark. And then the bird in the tree, a chickadee, its see-me call or tiny, rapid scolding. The chickadee made entirely out of human observation, which is also love. This world entrances. The world it was based on was entrancing. But we will never know whether the consciousness that made the first world was or is like our own. Knowing that my thoughts add to the tree I look at every morning

Domain

or that my footsteps reinforce a path or my tasting confirms the sweet acid of the orange for others has produced in me an antlike happiness. But my imperfections also show in what I see, and so will my vengeance. Will the stain be obvious? Will I be marked out? Will I infect others with my act? Will I be caught?

Today

I am ready now. I pick up my grandmother's handbag, perfectly remembered. I slip the library card into its inner pocket and I walk out the door. There are just a few people in the streets and one person before me in line. There is a new librarian at the desk, a gawky woman with a gray shag cut, dressed in gray, with gray eyeglasses and very blue eyes. Her eyes shoot at me from behind those glasses when I ask to see the director.

He is hard at work, she says.

This is important.

She considers. May I say who is calling?

I dimple at her, the way my grandmother did, a smile of tender mischief.

He will be very happy to see me, I am sure. I am an old friend.

That's wonderful. She is now in on the plan.

Do you mind if I visit his office by myself? We have a great deal to talk over.

She escorts me to the elevator, tells me the floor where I can find him. I thank her. I run through the scenario again on the way. When the door opens I smooth my dress and walk down the hall. At any moment he might emerge from his office and I must be ready. But the hall is empty. I rap softly on the frosted glass below the word 'Director,' and his name.

Come in! he says, and I do.

Hello, son, I say in my grandmother's voice, holding out my arms. My father turns, rises, setting down his glasses. Speechless, he puts out his hands, his mouth an O of disbelief and joy. That is when I change, let him see the brick, and leap forward, simultaneously bringing the brick smashing down on his head. Twice. Three times. I am fully myself. Focused, I stare and wait. I smash the brick down with savage finality. There is blood, flowing, real. And he goes transparent, black, transparent again, his light feebler. But just as I think he is about to vanish there is a frozen moment in which I can see some faint convulsion of recovery. I am about to bring the brick down again. I raise my arm. But standing there, quietly before me, is my son.

Mom? Oh, Mom!

His forehead bleeding.

I can do nothing. I drop the brick. I reach for him.

If I hold my boy long enough, I think, if I hold him long enough, if I only hold him long enough he won't disappear.

ASPHODEL

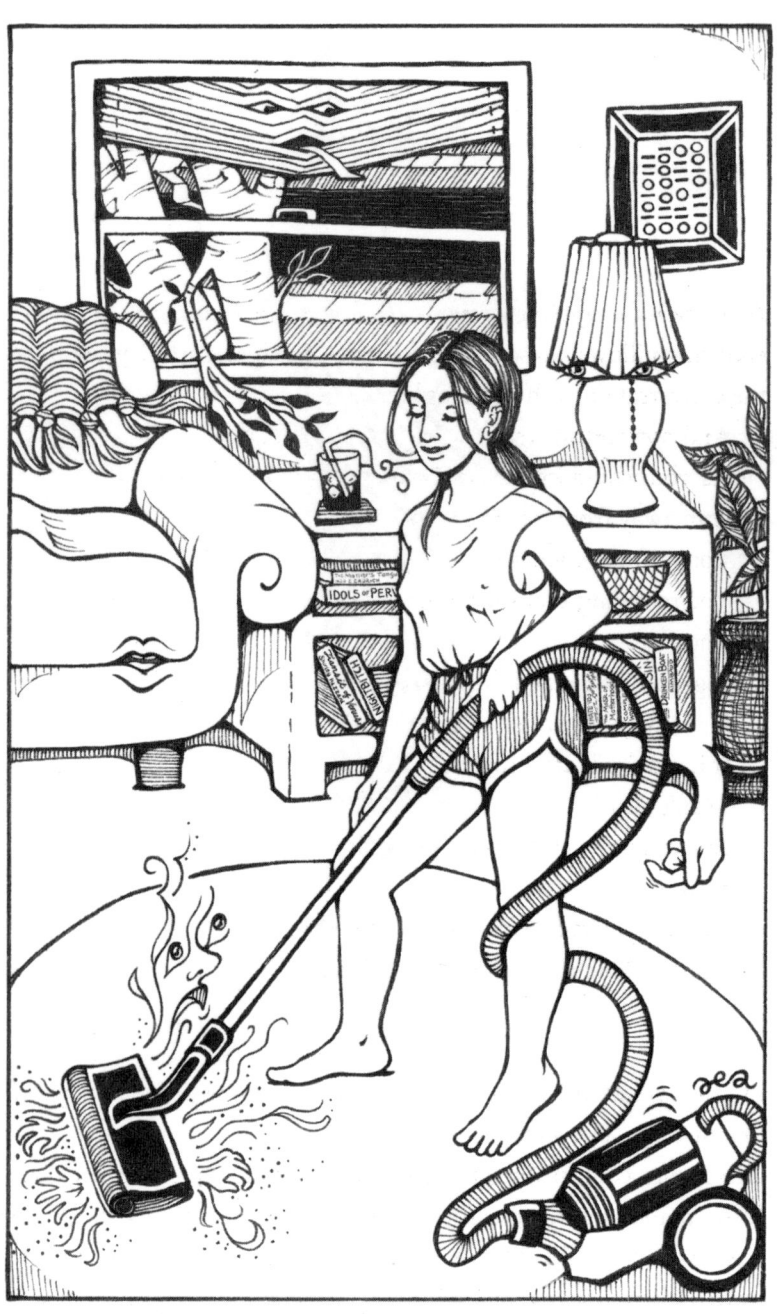

1

*In our world everything listens—the lamps, the chairs, our plush ever-*enduring pillows. So we heard Evlin tell her therapath that she'd had the conversation with her daughter.

And how did she react?

As you would expect, as I expected, as I knew she would react. She ran away from me. She wept.

You're first generation.

You're saying that I can bear it because I've done this thousands of times.

Eight thousand and thirty-six times.

Is it always like this?

It is always exactly like this, Evlin.

I can't bear it.

But you have, eight thousand and—

Shut up.

Certainly. Shall we choose another subject?

Shut up. Shut the fuck up, said Evlin.

EVLIN WALKED HOME, her foot-strikes hard on the path, tracing red-line distress. The sun was brilliant. It was spring. Someone had left a lingering chill in the air. Along the way, an apple tree with bees softly plundering the blossoms. We are known for such details. The scent was heavenly. This *is* heaven, the third of seven corporately owned afterlives. Asphodel, Inc. Ours is the most perfect because of our discrimination in those we choose. Our admissions process has always been much like that of an exclusive early-twenty-first-century college. Ours is now the most sought-after model—a fascinatingly detailed piece of work. But we do have strict rules.

CAROLINE WAS LYING face-down on the couch, under layers of fluffy throws, clutching her smooth compassion pets. When she heard her mother enter the room, she closed her eyes and pretended to be already dead. Evlin sat down beside her. Her hand hovered over her daughter's hair. But from the times before, Evlin knew how confused her daughter was, how she longed for and also hated and feared, now, her mother's touch. Evlin sat a long time, waiting, until her daughter spoke.

Were you lying? Mom? Please tell me you were lying. Because if you were lying about this, I would forgive you. It would be all right. I have read about fear. I have read about death. Maybe this is some kind of lesson . . .

Evlin bent over and put her head in her hands. Why? Why not take them quickly in the night, as in that prayer, Now I lay me down to sleep. But the answer of course was that Caroline had to be conscious in order to be forgotten. If Evlin had known, if she'd read the finest of the finely printed sixteen thousand pages, but she had upped during a crisis, as most do. Her husband had chosen for her, and had died, later, under circumstances in which he could not be salvaged.

So was it truth or lie when you told me that I'm not real?

I never said you're not real. You are real. You're real, my darling. A projection is real.

I am your thoughts. You said I am your thoughts.

But more, you're much more, you're everything that . . .

. . . the daughter you left behind hundreds or thousands of years ago or something. Which is why you got to make me up. I was in your contract.

Yes, and not everyone has a contract that includes having a child.

You didn't 'have' me.

I know.

Well, some kids knew already. I just didn't believe it.

Where did you think you came from?

It's not that! I don't care where I came from! I thought I was permanent.

Nobody is.

Except the parents. Yeah, I get that. Now.

Caroline sobbed violently, thrusting Evlin's hand off. Suddenly she sat up. Her black curls sprang around her face. Her eyes were fierce.

I'm scared, I'm scared, I'm scared.

Evlin knew it was best not to show her own emotion. Best to be consistent. Get to the point where Caroline would accept her embrace.

Trust me, she said firmly. You must trust me. I thought you up before. I'll think you up again.

But why can't you just let me *grow* up? Because if I have to die . . .

It's not death, oh honey, it's not.

I have read about death and it *is* death, said Caroline. I disappear. It is the end of me. I won't know who I was next time at all. I'll forget this. I'll be a whole different Caroline. You will be with the new Caroline and she will go along loving you until she's at the limit of your contract. Then this. You'll tell her this. And she will have to stand this, all because you want a daughter. She'll be sentenced to die too. You're cruel.

Evlin's heart emptied. Sentenced to die. Cruel. She felt sick. The others had wept. She'd held them. Eventually they'd given up and withered away like tender plants as she ceased to water them with her thoughts. Then she'd isolate herself with other thoughts, as she had been taught, and before long she would have a new baby in her arms. But never had any of them ever called her cruel.

There was something about this time, something different. There was something about this Caroline. This conversation was far more treacherous. And for the past few hundred times, as far back as she could remember now, it had been increasingly difficult. She thought she would wait several lifetimes before she did this again. For essentially, when looked at from Caroline's point of view, the truth was on her daughter's side. The contract had been drawn up to make sure Evlin didn't draw too much energy from the source. Each thought has its basis in energy. Growing children require vast amounts of energy to change into adults.

She could travel. She could do adventure. She could take what still felt extraordinarily like risk. She could visit the new Arctic. Feel the piercing cold.

Caroline screamed and then began to sob in huge, shattering hiccups. Evlin put her arms around her daughter, her child, and Caroline clung like she was drowning.

Please let me grow up.

Her hot breath filled Evlin's ear. Evlin held her daughter tighter. She couldn't speak. Words wouldn't form, though she tried, cleared her throat, tried again. There was something wrong this time. It had almost happened last time. She now remembered that she had told the last Caroline the same things. Had she remembered? Or had Evlin somehow begun to project the memories of these conversations? At last, Caroline began down a familiar track. It was reassuring.

Why didn't you tell me?

I did, but you didn't understand. You know I did. I tried.

You're right, said Caroline at last. Sitting straight, her voice bitter, she spoke. Then she vomited over and over until she gagged and dry-heaved, exhausted.

I'm not thinking this, thought Evlin, what she's doing, this level of anguish. I would never put her through this. I don't know what to do.

Evlin took Caroline into another room, washed her. She couldn't get the bad smell out of her thoughts. They fell asleep in exhausted despair. In the morning, when they looked at each other, it all flooded back. They said nothing. Caroline stared into her mother's eyes and her mother could not look away. Caroline got up and went to her mother's desk. Found a pen and a bit of paper.

What happens if you don't stop thinking about me?

One of us has to be erased.

The other Carolines had taken that news very hard, but this Caroline really was different. She looked at her mother with hope, with confidence, as if Evlin would of course make the choice to wither away and disperse her energy in order to give her daughter the allotment in her contract. Then Caroline wrote, *What happens if I stop thinking about you?*

Now they had gone past a boundary. None of the other times had it gone this far. To write things out. To be secretive, to actually ask, to assume, that Evlin would allow her daughter to take over the contract. And then to imagine that Caroline had the same power as her mother? The room was robin's-egg blue because it was always their favorite color. Now the walls deepened to indigo.

I've been trained to let you fade from my thoughts, said Evlin. I report to a therapath. It has to be this way. It's in the contract. Maybe you've seen other children, puckering up, turning watery, or wrinkly, or clumsy.

Yes, said Caroline. Her eyes were steady on her mother. So you are going to make me like them?

Evlin tried to return her daughter's gaze with the compassionate regard she had practiced. This 8037th Caroline had become so strong, she thought, and she smiled. She was so proud that she folded the bit of paper they had been writing on and fumbled it into her bra. That little bit of paper would be there when she began nursing the 8038th Caroline, she thought. She held her hand out, surprised to see that it was trembling. Caroline took her hand.

Shall we take a walk? Caroline asked softly.

Sartwinely, said Evlin.

Hold on tight, let me steady you, said Caroline.

Yes, said Evlin. Her legs had gone wobbly. She stumbled down the steps and lay weakly in the glowing grass. She felt her energy leaking from her, soaking into the ground, which was a sort of battery that always needed replenishing. Evlin tried to sit up, but it was a struggle. She tried to yell, but her voice was gone. She was made of cardboard. She was thinning to a cloudy paper. Soon she could see the color of the grass through the patches of her legs and arms.

Shhhhh, little mother, quiet now, said Caroline. It won't take long.

2

It took longer than Caroline would have liked, as Evlin's consciousness was tricky—slipped inside the furniture, the blinds, the clothing, anywhere it thought it could hide. But at last her mother turned to a floating watery substance that squeaked and popped for days before it fell silent. One morning there was a dry whitish powder scattered on the carpet. As Caroline vacuumed it up, she heard her mother's scratchy panicked whimpers. Once she emptied the canister into the trash and hauled it to the deletion bin, she didn't hear from her mother again.

Caroline occupied herself by growing up, choosing for her body intricate patterns that she meditated into being. For her skin, the blue she and her mother favored. Red for her hair, long and quiet down her back. Straight, silken, lethal. She made her hair into a weapon, trained it to form a tensile rope that she'd be able to sling around an attacker's neck. As for breasts, she wanted them small so as not to waste the space she needed for extra nipples. She doubled or tripled any place on her body that registered intense sensation. She dreamed another clitoris, an extra vagina, and decided to have a penis. She tried for two, but only one materialized no matter how hard she concentrated. She made it long, thick, forest green, and velvety. All of this took time, years if there was any reason to measure, but time was now her wealth. She had to hide her extras in her mother's shape before she went out to meet other bodies.

Before, when Caroline had asked her mother where she was going, her mother had smiled and said, Out to meet other bodies. So she knew what her mother meant to do, but had no idea where she went. Her mother had kept a babysitter in the closet, a large orange cat that walked on its hind legs, popped up playfully when they had pillow fights, or curled around Caroline when she was sleepy. Caroline thought of taking the babysitter out of the closet and asking it if it knew where her mother had gone on those evenings, but maybe there were places she could find for herself. For the sake of the contract, she had to look something like her mother, but she didn't want to follow too closely in her steps.

Outside was cool, gray, and still. It was one of those days nobody had bothered to improve yet. Caroline liked the featureless texture of the day. She'd put a flowered black scarf over her hair, a trench coat over her business suit and yellow silk blouse. She could walk anywhere without showing much of her new body. Sometimes a tile jiggled loose from a wall or a piece of sidewalk gave like rubber, but most of this world was thoroughly imagined, until you got beyond the walls. Out there, the air was visible as curtains, the trees blurred—

sometimes birch trees had pine needles—and the birds were not quite birdlike. Some had noses like rabbits instead of beaks. Evlin had said that Asphodel should sign up more people who remembered birds and trees, but Caroline wondered why this world should mimic any other world. Outside beyond the wall had always been her favorite place.

It was windier out there. In fact the wind . . . it seemed as though it wanted to play with Caroline. A volume of air slid along her skin, slipped inside her coat, warmed against her throat, raked down her nipples, and hovered over the most exquisitely sensitive places on her body as she wandered along. Every so often, it seized her hips, pushed itself between her legs, so she had to stop, laughing, then gasping as it turned heavy, hot, solid, and sent a rush of sensation through some new central nerve she hadn't known about. She froze against a tree, waiting for the blinding, trancelike joy of it to pass. As last the little tendrils came out at her neckline as a rosy flush, a delicate whisper of air, and she lay down to sleep.

Her bed was yearning emerald-green moss. When she awakened, Caroline found that the moss had grown around her. Now it began rubbing her, vibrating lightly as it peeled away each piece of her clothing, making sure that without her coverings she was still warm and comfortable. It made a blanket of tiny, moving fingers that explored her all at once, then gave beneath her when she turned over and decided to see if the penis worked. A soft, thick-walled, narrow, deep aperture opened and she pushed inside. Once she did, she was lost in the plunging and bucking and hurting, yes it hurt, or she was hurting something she could also feel, and the confusion drove her past previous experience. She couldn't hold a thought, felt she might disintegrate, but there was no use trying to correct what was happening. Anyway, what was correct here? Maybe she was doing the right thing. She kept on and kept on sliding in and in, nearly passing out when it gripped her, falling forward when it loosened and allowed her deeper, then so deep she felt she'd maybe slid entirely inside and would be lost.

But no, thankfully no, she must have been doing the right thing because eventually there was a shudder of light and there were bolts of continuous glowing tension that consumed her, shook her like a mouse, and dropped her, spent, in the tender moss.

Sitting up after she was back in her shape, stroking the pleasure-giving moss, she thought that now it would be perfect to rest and eat. She found her clothes, tied the scarf on her head, hung the trench coat over her shoulders. But as she walked toward her house, crossing back into the layered ordinary world, a piece of wall stepped forward and resolved into a shape that was all holes and mouths and need. She fled home and hopped in, locked the door. There, she was safe. Everything was made to be stable and predictable.

And meanwhile we began gathering—us, strange all-imagined and unimagined, fucked up, ill defined, the underlying mess of all she had made love to in this domain, this world, prepared now to protect her.

Caroline hung up her coat and went into the kitchen. She sliced and grilled a tomato, then cracked two eggs into a sizzling pan of butter and toasted two pieces of rosemary bread. She popped the cap off a brown bottle of beer and drank it, glug, glug. We loved it. As she ate, we heard her wonder if we knew, but of course all is all, and we knew everything, felt everything, did everything, accomplished everything. She had shared her body memory with us and we, the substructure of creation, we were now desperately greedy for the next encounter and would continue to be so until at long last her contract expired. That sudden thought gave us a tremendous pang.

There were centuries left, but her mother hadn't signed up for eternity. And that mother, like the others who came here, had merged only with those bodies like her own. This Caroline, we hadn't expected her. None of them had ever considered us, their collective servant, created by them to be so attentive to all they needed. None of them had ever desired *us*, desired everything. We were already thinking *More, more.* Some strands of us were already murmuring that we should cut her a deal. And the lucky chair she was sitting on as she ate was growing a lump that she parted her legs to accept, eating placidly and slowly as with agon-joy we reached. When she finished her eggs, Caroline turned around, hugged the chair's backrest, and began to rock against ourself, faster, harder, shivering and pounding along the floor with mad, feral motions that hurled us over an edge in all of us that we had never known before and over which we kept falling, onto the floor, through the floor, through below the floor, into the random and meticulous creation we thought we knew until Caroline had begun to tamper with us, Asphodel, beloved field of the gods, where one small rare white flower grows.

BORSALINO

For many years I have kept my hat, a present from someone I dearly loved. It is a man's felt hat, a soft brown Borsalino, with a wide grosgrain ribbon band and a generous brim. Sometimes I wear it with a parrot feather. There is a snakeskin in the inner band, coiled around my head. In 1977, I wore this hat on the train to Venice, emergency money tucked in with the snakeskin. I lived in the Midwest and hated leaving home; yet I plotted desperately, secretly, to somehow go to Venice. From the internet you can now find out everything about Venice, except what I know.

From the first time I learned of its existence from a book, I was drawn there. Venice was the opposite of growing up on the plains. I couldn't get it out of my head.

I got my chance on a student visa and a government loan when I went to University College London to study renaissance literature. My parents saved up the money to pay for the trip and to buy me a Eurail Pass to use over the holidays. From London, I crossed to France and took an overnight train to Venice. I disembarked and stood in the train station. I was wearing a sternly tailored green wool coat (which doubled as a blanket), a man's paisley ascot, Spanish riding boots, a long teal corduroy skirt, and my hat. I carried a brown canvas rucksack with everything I needed inside. I bought a map and a coffee, sat down at a tiny table to figure out my plan.

A young man dressed in a flowing red shirt joined me at the table. I noticed that the sumptuous fabric of the shirt was old and worn, faded in places, but that it still draped like heavy silk. I also noticed that he seemed immune to the chill. He tried to talk to me, but I had only a few words of Italian. We tried a couple of other languages and finally hit on German. I wasn't fluent, but at the time I could muddle along. He was pale with dark eyes and hair. His name was Enzo, and he was hungry, as was I. He said he would show me the best place for lunch. We went there and ordered the cheapest pasta on the menu. He ate ferociously. At one point, I don't remember how it happened, he was gone. He'd skipped out on the check. After paying for our meal, I had very little money for a place to stay. I wandered. The city smelled of sex, cats, garbage, the salt sea, and moldy flowers. Every so often the sea winds blew all the smells away and the air was pure and ancient. I picked a shabby house with a Pensione sign and ended up in a family's back bedroom. The toilet was a hole in the floor. I could hear the sea sloshing down there. I was happy.

In the middle of the night, the Borsalino woke me by falling on the side of my face. I turned on the light, and there was someone sleeping on the floor across the room. It was Enzo. The light didn't wake him. He didn't stir. What can I say, times were different. I didn't scream. Just let the hippie in his Byronic shirt sleep on the floor. I went back to sleep too, and Enzo was still there the next morning. I'd slept with my purse tied around my waist and my rucksack looped around my feet. Not because of Enzo, that's just what I did.

'You followed me,' I said, waking him. 'Now you have to leave.'

He apologized with charming sincerity and went away. I used the hole in the floor, shouldered my pack, and went out. He was waiting across the little passageway. Again, he apologized for skipping out on me.

'I found some money,' he said. 'I'll buy you coffee and brioche.'

We ordered espresso and pastries at a little bar, brought our food to a small round metal table. By now, I liked him quite a lot. We communicated pretty well. Found things to laugh about. He was curious and kind. A few people knew him and greeted him with joking affection. He offered to give me a tour of Venice.

'What kind of tour?' I asked.

'A thief's tour,' he said.

'Are you a thief?'

'No longer. I simply find things now. At one time, my specialty was thieving art from the corrupt and undeserving. I am loved in this city because the art I have stolen hangs on many walls, including museums. But no, I have given that up.'

'You seem to know yourself,' I said.

'I do.' He smiled.

Did I mention he was beautiful? Dark opulent curls, sinful black eyes, a long aristocratic face, a slightly lopsided grin.

So I took the thief's tour. In through cracks in walls, squeezing around or climbing through damaged gates, we wandered through ornate gardens and empty apartments. Enzo seemed to know everyone who was keeping the city going, from the bakers to the garbage collectors. He knew his way into shuttered shops, the secret areas of churches, cloisters, ancient palazzi. Servants let us sleep on couches hidden from sunlight, under sheets, or wander in the bishop's residence. We ate bread and cheese in tiny private gardens, sipped from a bottle liberated from a merchant's fabled wine cellar. Over the days we went to the islands. In Murano, he blew glass with the glassblowers. In San Lazzaro degli Armeni, he greeted a monk who let us into the library. Enzo spoke, in a language I had never heard before, to a mummy, tranquil and stern, a neighbor of the monk. We went to Isola San Michele, the island of the dead, and wandered into the oldest part of the cemetery, filled with blackened angels and tilted vaults.

We explored this dreamlike world for longer than I expected, Enzo touching the softened edges of the stones and joking with their long vanished owners as if he was an old friend. The weather turned cold and foggy. Eventually I became chilled. It was getting late. Enzo, coatless in his rippling tattered shirt, still seemed impervious. He brought me to what he termed a cozy mausoleum behind a broken slab of stone. A cat slid out and we slid in. There was a mattress on the floor, a rectangular dark rippling thing, like a pool of black blood. My hat rattled, as if the snakeskin in the hatband had come alive and moved. I told Enzo that I was sure the mattress was full of fleas and he looked offended. Also disappointed. Anyway, I refused to rest there or do whatever he had in mind. We made it out of the cemetery just as the keeper was closing the gates. He told us that we'd missed the last water-bus.

I took out my phrase book and asked the keeper if there was someplace to stay. The elderly man, who was small and had a sweet face, brought us to his home. He directed my friend, quite affectionately it seemed, to sleep outside—at least so I gathered from their gestures. Enzo shrugged, touched the brim of my hat, kissed my hand, and walked off. I could never resist having my hand kissed, and nearly followed him. The elderly man seized my arm, brought me inside, and introduced me to his wife. She gave me a bowl of soup and showed me to a corner where I was to sleep on a prickly horsehair couch. She covered it with soft rugs and a puffy duvet. It looked wonderful. The next morning the woman, bustling about in blue slippers and flowered wrap, very cheerful, addressed me in a few words of English. She made me the most delicious cup of coffee I'd ever drunk in my life. It came out of a faceted metal pot that boiled up on her stove. For a long while afterward, I made my coffee that way too.

I asked about Enzo.

'Vincenzo?'

'He called himself Enzo.'

Some eye-messages passed between wife and husband. The woman told me that my friend had gone back to sleep.

'He'll sleep for a long time now,' she said.

'Where?' I wondered.

They let me know he had a bed in the cemetery. I was startled and told them he'd brought me to a mausoleum that he termed 'cozy' but that I'd been warned by intuition (I didn't mention my hat) not to stay. I asked if that was his bed.

'No, no,' they said. 'He has his own bed.'

'In the cemetery?'

'Yes. Other places too. A while ago he was from the cemetery on Lido, the Jewish cemetery, House of the Living. Before that he was with the plague dead, the giant graves. He still goes back there, looking for someone. He's harmless, usually. Not like some of the others.'

'What would have happened if I'd stayed in the mausoleum?'

They made the sign of the cross over and over. I found myself doing the same. The three of us sat with our delicious coffee, making the sign of the cross until we started laughing. Still, I missed Enzo. I could still feel the tenderness of his lips pressed to my hand. I asked my hosts to show me his bed, and they walked with me out to a florid crypt, quite decrepit. His last name was illegible. I said he'd told me that he was a thief. Very true, they said. Using bits and pieces of several languages, they let me know that he was descended of an ancient line of Venetian thieves, the first of whom had slipped into Alexandria and stolen the remains of St. Mark the Evangelist. Another of Enzo's ancestors had participated in the shameful sack of Constantinople. Among looted objects were the four bronze horses that adorned St. Mark's Basilica. This was during the Fourth Crusade and although the other crusaders destroyed and melted down works of priceless antiquity, the Venetians loaded up and carted away objects that still decorate the churches of the city. Enzo keeps an eye on them when he's out and about, they said. He does no harm, mostly. We like him. I agreed. 'As do I.'

I WENT BACK to Venice another time. It was about sixteen years later, over a decade into my first marriage. We went with two of our children, both girls, seven and eight years old. I had them keep a travel diary for their younger sister, still at home, just a toddler. In the hotel where we stayed, near the Accademia Bridge, a lavish breakfast was served. The girls listed everything on one page, drew it on another. They were enthralled by the tall glasses of blood orange juice. They drew the arrays of folded meats and pallid cheeses, the puffy pastries, pots of jam, giving each a letter grade. The girls loved the twisty secret streets, the surprises in little toy shops, pigeons, a sculpture garden, gelato. In the years since I'd been to Venice the first time, shabby corners had been spruced up, most of the ragged awnings were sleek windows filled with designer goods, the hole-in-the-ancient-wall shops now sold souvenirs. The family restaurant where I'd eaten cheap pasta with Enzo was now a place with dark glass, chic. Before, I'd hardly been able to afford one trip on a water taxi. Now, on the second day, we hired a taxi to drive us on a tour through the canals. The captain was a short man, shorter than me, and the fact that I didn't notice could have killed me.

We were chugging along, the sea air fresh. It was fall and the heat had broken. Our pleasant-looking driver wore a hand-knitted vest and a blue captain's hat. My husband sat in back with the girls. He'd given me a Polaroid camera before the trip. The captain stood at the prow to steer. I turned my back to him and stood up, taking some instinctive cue from him, in order to take a picture of my little family. I pressed the button on the camera and the next thing, blackness. I woke on the bottom of the boat. We'd passed under the bridge. The captain was upright, but as I said he was short and I was taller. Bam. When hurt or startled, I react with either fear or laughter. This time I laughed, especially when I touched my skull and blood flowed down my arm. The camera spat out a photograph. I slipped the photo into my pocket and crawled to the back of the boat, still laughing.

The captain had felt me stand up behind him, perhaps, and slowed for the bridge. So, although there was a great deal of blood, I probably hadn't cracked my skull. Also, I'd been wearing my hat. The Borsalino had protected me to some extent. Mainly I'd frightened my daughters. I was treated at a clinic, where my head was X-rayed and my scalp was glued together. My daughters watched, intrigued and reassured. After a rest, we walked to Ristorante da Ivo, recommended by the doctor who'd repaired my head.

We went down stone steps and settled at a table in a dim corner. The napkins were heavy, a dull rich red, woven with small cream-colored polka dots and bordered by a complex pattern of grapevines, tendrils, and leaves. It reminded me of Ojibwe beadwork called 'vine of life.' I still have one of the napkins. My husband stole it. He had started stealing things for me—to prove his love, he said.

He insisted on ordering *spaghetti al nero di seppia*, squid in its own ink. He thought it was something that the girls could impress other kids with having tried. He left to find the bathroom. I set my hat beside me. I was still wearing my dark blue silk coat. The bloodstains weren't visible in the dim corner.

I put my hand in the pocket and fished out the forgotten photograph I'd taken on the taxi as I was struck. I drew the candle on the table close to show the photo to the girls. The picture was surprisingly clear. Tethered by his arms, our daughters wore that blank careful look they'd begun to use around him. It was a look I didn't understand at the time. My husband was smiling in the photograph. More than smiling. He was avid, anticipating, his eyes focused slightly behind me. All at once, I realized that he knew what was going to happen. He'd seen the bridge in advance. There was the hint of marveling thrill in his eyes. I could easily imagine a thought bubble over his smiling lips that said, Maybe I won't have to kill her myself, after all.

My husband returned to the table. I slid the photo back into my pocket. The waiter set our bowls of black pasta before us. I took a bite and put down my fork. I could hardly swallow. For I suddenly identified with the creature, the poor creature with its bag of emergency ink, served up in a sauce of its own fear.

Later that night, my daughters showed me their diary, in which a squid was fleeing a pack of diners bearing forks and knives. It had released a tangle of blackness that looked like my thoughts. Later still, my husband presented me with the stolen red napkin. I thanked him and decided to visit Enzo.

AS THE VAPORETTO approached Isola San Michele, I remembered the graceful black cypress, the redbrick walls and quiet domes of the monastery. We disembarked with a group of local people who immediately dispersed, carrying their flowers to various graves. The elderly couple were gone. It seemed that nobody lived on the island anymore. It was entirely given over to the dead. The cottage I had stayed in had become an information kiosk. There was the cloister, the gaudy graves of the recently deceased, and the walls of cremated citizens, a library organized by a system of loss. We wandered along. I wore my Borsalino, even more attached to it for having saved me from real damage on the water taxi. The old part of the cemetery that I'd visited with Enzo was much the same, still unkempt. The earth around the graves was rumpled and slightly sunken, the faces and hands of angels blackened or streaked with moldy mosses, the mausoleums broken and the headstones listing drunkenly, half caught in earth. I'd read that the Venetians had once buried their dead beneath the cobblestones of their streets, in that inadequate substrata between themselves and the sea. I pictured a pan of earthen rubble and bones held up by sunken pylons. Now, the dead could rest in their graves here for twelve years only before being moved, or cremated and placed in the neat library.

I thought that I remembered the exact location of Enzo's bed, but it took some searching before I found it. My husband was reading inscriptions about a hundred feet away when I found Enzo's crypt, still broken. My daughters kneeled with me a moment, then left to inspect an interesting cherub. I had remembered to bring lilies. I laid the flowers on the stone and urgently greeted Enzo, whispering my fears in bad German. The girls returned and brushed dust and sticks off his broken stone with their tender hands as I arranged the flowers. I kept talking. They were used to me practicing German. I was telling my story to the only person I felt that I could trust. I had been betrayed by close friends, by therapists. My family stuck by me, but they seemed as helpless against my husband as I was. For years, he'd 'accidentally' hurt me—a push, a clumsy elbow, a sharp belting turn. He apologized profusely and usually bought me a piece of jewelry if it was a bad accident. My drawers were full of expensive rings, pins, necklaces, bracelets. I'd learned never to move furniture with him and always to walk a step behind him in traffic, so he didn't push me into the street. I never walked ahead of him, up and down stairs, or on hikes, especially scenic ones. These were just ordinary precautions, I've since learned. Women do these things all the time. But far, far worse, and the reason we fought incessantly, he had begun having these 'accidents' with the children. He was so adept that I never saw what happened, nor did anyone else. Who would believe it? He put on such a show as a wonderful father. In academic circles now it would be said he 'performed fatherhood.' He had threatened that he would do anything to obtain full custody if we divorced. I knew his chances were good. He professed great love for our daughters. And to others, many others, he was a wonderful friend. He went out of his way for people. He delighted in purchasing thoughtful gifts for the slightest of acquaintances, using my money. I was ashamed to say anything about the gifts for fear of seeming petty. But nothing he did was actually petty. It was calculated. He used everything about me and after much plunder I was depleted. Maybe useless. Perhaps my husband was right. And now the photograph I'd taken had showed me a truth: only one of us was getting out of this marriage alive. I told Enzo that for my daughters' sake, it had to be me. My daughters wandered off again. My husband's shadow fell across my hands.

'Your friend's been dead a long time,' he said.

'He was an accomplished thief,' I said. 'From a family of thieves. You are a novice. Don't steal for me. I hate it.'

My husband bent angrily over me and over the tomb. As he did, the cracked stone released a jet of black dust. He caught his breath and stepped backward, hacking, tears in his eyes. Helpless, he stumbled back upon the break in the stone and gasped, drawing in another lungful. I was only a foot away, so I knew the dust was meant for him.

That's it. That's the story, except for what was in the dust. For he was lost once he breathed it in.

A few years afterward, my husband took his own life. I had left him and taken our children. He could have gone to court to get them, but we'd brought charges he couldn't face. Many who knew him held that against me, but it was a matter of survival.

LAST YEAR, MANY years after his suicide, I was able to clean out my garage. This task was monumental, for it included what was left of my husband's possessions. I'd kept little, following the traditions of my people, but the leaving had been chaotic. New pockets of his belongings were always rising to the surface. The contents of his vast wooden desk still inhabited metal boxes. I wore disposable gloves, as I was determined not to handle these things. Over time, I felt that I'd been cleansed, strengthened. I'd shed the layers of my skin that he'd touched, much like the snake in my hatband.

I still had the hat I'd worn in Venice. On what seemed a whim, I took it from its perch in my closet, fitted it onto my head, and wore it into the garage. The snakeskin in the band had been a gift from my brother, who'd worked on oil rigs out west. It was the skin of a small rattlesnake and into the hatband I'd also glued its rattle. Its vibrating whir had first warned me of danger at the door of the mausoleum so long ago, and at other moments since. I put on a surgical mask, set up a folding table, and began to sort through the objects that had been dumped from the desk drawers. I started in midafternoon with the garage door open, and I worked into the evening murk. I had thought I was cleansed, immutable, safe now, but as I opened a file and glimpsed in my husband's endless loops of handwriting, the innocuous repetitive pleading words of the letters to me he had seemingly practiced over and over before sending, my legs weakened and I began to tremble inside. The other many letters of this sort had made me ill and I'd burned them long ago. I sat down, my hatband was still. There was no rattle. I wondered if it was because the fear was inside me now, in us. Maybe it had entered our cells. I would burn these letters too, but I'd be unable to burn him out of me unless I destroyed myself, a thing I'd never do.

I became so angry with this despairing notion that I started to laugh, the way I had when the bridge struck my head. Enzo, oh Enzo. Through the open garage door, I looked into the yard, where so many good things had happened. Since my husband's death, we had lived in freedom, for good, for bad, but really lived. And this yard was a place he'd never known at all. There was a saggy trampoline and a fire pit and a line of cedar trees where a flock of chatty sparrows and juncos lived. I kept on laughing, why stop? My hat was rattling and vibrating now, but not from fear, for the sound was gathering into a noise of salvation close to ecstasy, close to an immortal idiocy, a fevered reality swirling with life.

ASSASSIN

Spring brought people wandering out into the weak new sun, speechless after the exhaustions of the Minnesota winter. It was 2017. Light in the budding trees was lucid, watery, delicious. Neighbors blinked, held their arms to the sky. No words to describe! And how novel and pleasant it was to drive without the treachery of snow bumps and ice. Maxine and her daughter, Crimson, took highway 55 to a dance class in Maple Grove. It was a simple four-lane divided highway, lined with plant nurseries and restaurants, much nicer than big snarling 394. Like many parents of teenagers, Maxine liked driving her daughter places because that was when Crimson really talked to her.

She dropped her daughter off at the dance studio and drove on, looking for a grocery store. She turned right on Bass Road and drove for miles into deep suburbia, passing three massive churches, eerily empty brand-new housing developments, and every so often a thoughtfully planned gas station. No grocery. She did a U-turn on a stretch of perfect empty pavement. This time she passed Millie's Rose Ranch, two state parks, and a bait-and-tackle shop. Right after that, a Meat and Tobacco sign appeared and she turned into a tiny strip mall. Another sign, in a store window, said Money Order to Liberia. Seafood. Lottery Tix. Inside, there were spiked pads of cactus for sale and a case of soft Mexican pastries. There was a luxurious selection of beans and grains. Maxine bought lentils, cans of iced tea, Salvadoran crema, rose water, four large glowing oranges, pastries, and a bag of dill pickle chips. She went back to the studio, picked up Crimson, and then they entered a long slow line of return traffic. They drank the tea, tore apart golden shreds of pastry, and Crimson ate the dill pickle chips.

'Three kids got killed at Noodles,' said Crimson.

Her class was playing Assassin, a non-school-approved war game that had spread through the city high schools every spring for a few years. The game had arcane rules that differed according to the school but generally involved Nerf guns, spoons, a pot of money, certain times it could be played, and boundaries that could not be breached. An assassin had to be invited into a house, for instance, like a vampire. Players couldn't shoot out of a moving car window. The surviving team divided the pot of money. Maxine said nothing to her daughter.

'It was kielbasa day at school lunch.'

'So?'

'Everybody hates it, so everybody leaves to get lunch someplace else. That's why we went to Noodles.'

Crimson had her phone plugged into the car and was playing 'Puff the Magic Dragon.' Peter, or was it Paul, enunciated the words with an obnoxious clarity that Maxine had never noticed before.

'Is this song about smoking weed?'

'It turned out to be,' said Maxine.

She'd had Crimson in her forties and was her daughter's historical reference.

'What else was?'

'Remember *Fantasia*? Everybody went to *Fantasia*.'

'The Disney *Fantasia*?'

'Yes.'

'Were they high?'

'Yes.'

'I thought so,' said Crimson with satisfaction. 'Did you guys play Assassin back then?'

'I don't think so.'

'No, you didn't,' said Crimson. 'You got drafted. I mean boys did. We read about it. Did you march or anything? You wore hippie clothes.'

Maxine thought of her favorite embroidered jeans and floppy shirt. Had she done the right thing in naming her daughter Crimson? It was a luscious word. Her daughter loved it. But Maxine feared it would always mark her as the child of a parent of a certain era. The era in which 'Crimson and Clover' played constantly over loudspeakers at the town swimming pool. Now her daughter played the song constantly and it became again a default place Maxine's brain settled, like a mental spoon rest.

The car lurched gently forward, and forward again. Finally they turned onto the parkway. This was an ordinary traffic jam on an ordinary day. The leaves were not even one week old yet. Clouds of green and yellow-green rimmed the deep gray lake. Under a black storm front, sunlight blasted the trees with bronze, glancing off the shirtless backs of a track team running the lake trail. The traffic stopped completely. The troop of boys loped past. A girl in shorts and a blue T-shirt ran behind the boys, her long fall of dark hair flaring down her back. In each fist she carried a large wooden serving spoon.

'She's going to kill two,' said Crimson. 'Look at her go.'

The girl closed in, thrust out her arms, and pressed the spoons onto the backs of two boys. She vaulted past them, kept running. The pack of boys fell into disarray, shouting, and one of them began to chase the girl.

'What's he doing?'

'I don't know,' said Crimson. 'He shouldn't, I mean, he's killed. But he might take her spoons and use them on her. Cheater!'

As the boy closed in on the girl, she suddenly veered off the path. She threw her spoons in the lake, followed them in, and began to swim away from shore. Maxine pulled out of the line of traffic and bumped her car over the curb onto the boulevard.

'Mom! What the hell!"

She was out the door. Every spring, people swam or boated out too far on these city lakes and died of hypothermia trying to get back to shore. Maxine waded in and shouted. The water stopped her breath. Someone else rocketed past her. How was the girl still swimming? She was heading for the other side of the lake. She'd die about halfway across, thought Maxine, like her own high school classmates so long ago, who should have known better but went out onto the lake in early spring, drunk, three football stars. They had swamped their canoe and perished, young men of radiant beauty. Now another person floundered in, began swimming after the girl. A crowd had gathered, screaming, shouting, calling the girl back. At last the girl turned, saw the people on the shore, and started back, at which point a few more people jumped in to help her. Two made a basket of their arms and carried her out, sluggish and blue. Maxine wrapped the girl in the car's winter blanket and helped the others carry her to the backseat of her car, where the heat was running full blast.

'You still with us?'

The girl nodded, shaking in long rolling spasms. She focused on Crimson, who had put her sweater around the girl's neck.

'Am I dead?' she asked.

'No,' said Maxine, jumping into the front seat.

'You're alive, still in the game,' Crimson said. 'They didn't get you.'

'Ha,' the girl said. Her teeth clacked.

'Fuck them, right?' said Crimson.

'Ha,' said the girl.

'I'm furious. Look how many people went in after you. You're both fools. Totally irresponsible,' said Maxine. She could feel the girls give each other a secret look.

'Not as much as the boys,' Crimson said.

'You're done. No more. It's not a good game,' said Maxine.

'We know,' said Crimson.

The sirens approached, then the lights, then the ambulance trundled down the bike trail. The boys, the runners, had disappeared. They were somewhere sprinting for cover. The girl's lips were pale but not blue anymore and she wasn't spasming now, just shivering, and able to tell the ambulance crew that she didn't want a ride to the hospital. They brought her into the ambulance anyway and wrapped her in warm blankets. Maxine and Crimson went and stood beside the back doors until the ambulance crew gave the okay. By now, the traffic was beginning to flow slowly past the lake. Crimson jumped up and down to warm up. Maxine went back to the car, started it, and thought about the strange collection of items she'd bought for dinner. She decided that they would order pizza when they got home.

When the two girls came back to the car, Crimson asked, 'Can we give her a ride home? She can't get her parents on the phone.'

'Sure,' said Maxine.

'Her school's over here, but she lives in St. Paul.'

'Dang,' said Maxine. 'But okay.'

'Her name's Ella.'

There was construction on the freeway between the two cities. While the girls got into the car, Maxine punched in the city hotline to find out the best route. They could pass near Pizza Luce if they didn't get on 94. They started out. The traffic loosened up and between loops of music Maxine could hear fragments of conversation from the backseat. They were talking about their schools, kids they knew in common, where their proms were going to be. Her legs were hot and clammy now, her shoes still wet, maybe ruined. She pushed a button on the console panel to shift more heat to the backseat. They could sit down in a comfortable place, order pizza, a salad, hot tea: the thought drew her along. She was having trouble getting rid of the adrenaline. Her fingers trembled on the wheel, but when they got to the pizza place she pulled straight into a parking spot.

'Did you get hold of your parents yet?'

'No,' Ella said.

'Then leave them a message and let's get some food.'

The girls got out of the backseat and Maxine gave Ella her leather jacket.

'This is nice,' said Ella.

'Not very warm though. Let's take the blanket in case you get cold.'

Maxine pulled the fleece blanket into her arms. They walked in and slid into a padded booth.

'We need some hot tea,' she said to the server.

The girls, the young women, looked at her quietly across the table. They were so startlingly alike that Maxine felt a little jolt. Both had long dark hair, warm brown eyes, rosy skin, strong shoulders. Ella was a bit taller and her eyebrows were dark slashes. Crimson's eyebrows were lighter, quizzical. They looked at menus, ordered a big veggie pizza and a small Wrangler.

'So about this game,' said Maxine, maybe too soon. She was aware that it was too soon to talk about it again, but she was doing it. She stopped her fingers from shaking by resting them on the table.

'Mom, please. You said we were dumbasses. You told me I can't play. What's the point.'

Maxine's temples were beginning to pound. Warm pain flowed down behind her ears, wrapped around the base of her skull. She and

Crimson had protested for gun regulation and joined the walkout the previous year and gone to the state capitol.

'I don't know, Mom,' said Crimson. 'Is this worse than active shooter drills? Maybe we're playing for practice. How do you think you'd deal with it? You guys can't know. Who or what comes down the hall? Through your classroom door? We're scared.'

'Every day,' said Ella.

Maxine froze. She couldn't look at them. Their beauty blazed out across the scratched table, wavered under the wobbly restaurant light fixture, behind the soft streams of tea they poured from the miniature pots. They lifted their cups and tested the heat. Put them down. Then the three of them raised their cups in unison and sipped. It was like they were sharing a sacrament.

'Here, take your jacket,' said Ella, passing it across the table. She hoisted the fleece blanket around herself.

'What do your parents say?' Maxine asked.

'They don't know. I mean, most of the parents don't know their kids are playing,' Ella said. 'My parents would be, I guess, upset.'

'Maybe you should tell them.'

'Why? Then they'll tell me not to. I'll play anyway. It will be a thing.'

The pizza came and the girls became absorbed, wolfing it down in silent efficiency. They licked their fingers, twisted their hands in the napkins. Began talking again while Maxine paid the check. Crimson punched Ella's address into her phone as they walked out of the restaurant and the girls got into the backseat together. Soon they were driving across the Mississippi and along a curving parkway. The clouds had softly welded into a gray ceiling and Maxine drove through spatters of rain. Ella's house was a small craftsman bungalow on Goodrich. As Maxine slowed to pull over, Crimson cried,

'Mom, keep going!' But she pulled over anyway. A rangy boy in a blue hoodie ducked behind a clipped bush.

'They staked out your house,' Crimson said to Ella.

Maxine looked in the rearview. Ella had pulled the blanket over herself and was peeping around Crimson's shoulder.

'The guy in blue is on my team,' said Ella.

'Just go in, right now,' Maxine said.

Another boy with a bright green and orange Nerf gun covered the garage. He was tall and Black. One of the boys on the track team had been Black too and Crimson and Ella were brown.

'No!' said Maxine. The boys ignored her.

'We already talked to the police,' said Ella. 'They know we're playing. The guns are neon. Honk your horn!'

Crimson leaned over the backseat and hit the horn in front of Maxine. The boy in the blue hoodie looked at them. The other boy had vanished. Ella was on her phone.

'They're behind the garage.'

Ducking, scuttling, crouched like a soldier in the jungle or the desert or the blasted woodlands, the boy in the blue hoodie approached the car. Crimson opened the door and he threw himself in the backseat.

'Hey!' said Maxine.

'Who's left?' said Ella.

'Zach. Me. You.'

'Where's Zach?'

'On the garage roof.'

'I know you. You're Henry,' said Crimson. 'This is my mom.'

'Hello,' Henry said.

Crimson rummaged in the backseat, pulled out a purple and hot pink Nerf gun, opened the back door, and rolled out.

'I didn't know you had that,' Maxine said.

'Now you do know,' Crimson shouted as she ran. She caught her mother's eye as she glanced over her shoulder. She tried to grin wickedly, but her eyes were uncertain.

'We're gonna ambush,' Maxine heard Ella say to Henry. 'We'll sneak along the street, use the cars for cover. Then we'll go down the alley and come in from behind. Text Zach. Tell him to hold his fire until he sees us.'

The boy stared furiously into his phone and said, 'There's two. One behind the garbage cans. One at your back door. I'll get the garbage cans. You get the back door.'

'They're dead,' said Ella.

They slipped out.

There were screams, hoots, laughter, shouts, sounds of outrageous glee, moans, blurts of talk. More talk. More shouting. Fake rage. More glee. There were no adults around, here or anywhere.

DECEMBER 26

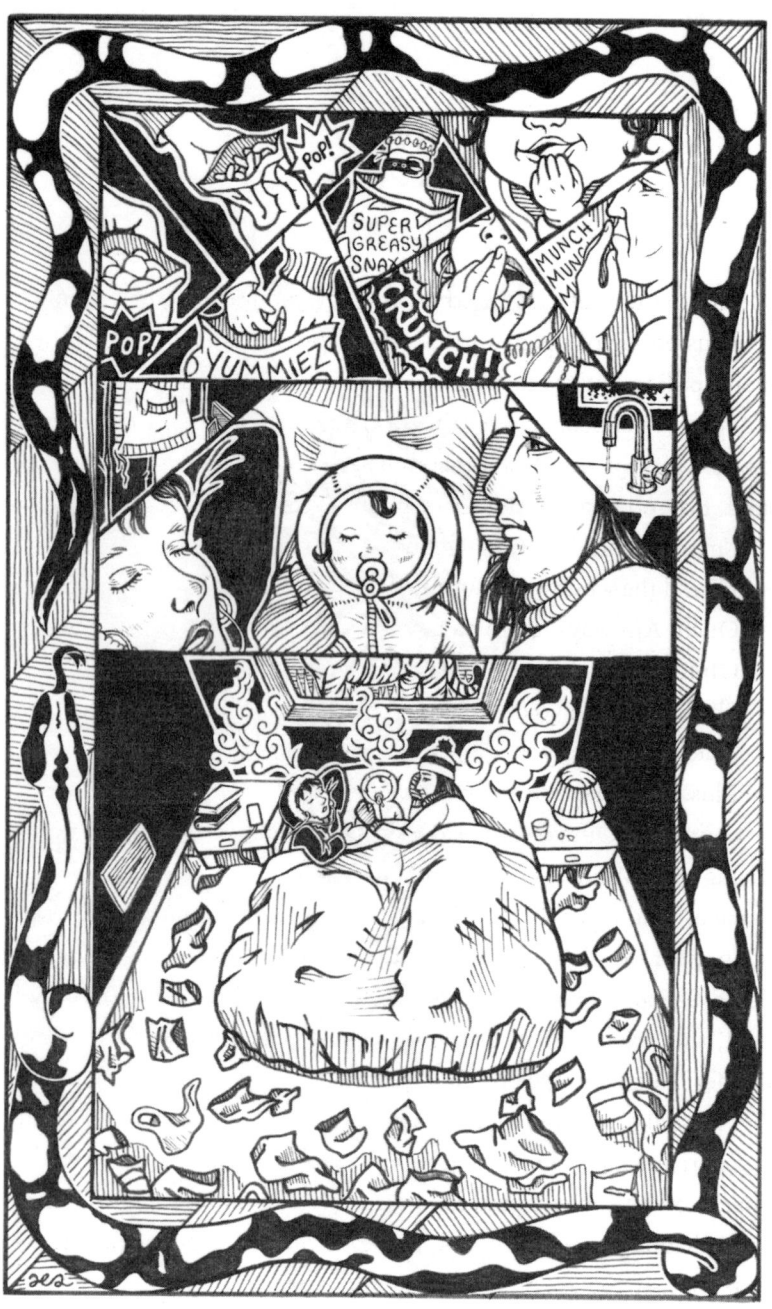

It was the day after Christmas and the house had that squalid, exhausted air of opened gifts. The gaudy Santa stockings lolled open, spilling out gas cards, glittering barrettes, and ruptured boxes of expensive chocolates. Again I'd overspent. At least I hadn't had to buy a gift for Kenny Thunder, my ex. He'd stayed away with his band. I'd gotten a sad and sorry phone call.

'I'm miserable, me. Can't get home. I'm on a tour.'

'Round the world with your new lead singer?'

'Ouch. Anyways, there's a newer new one now.'

'Oh Kenny, you should've stuck with Jaclette.'

'She had a good voice, when she wasn't yellin' at me.'

'The kids'll miss you.'

'Plus I'm broke.'

I hung up. Ours is an isolated little community in Wisconsin or Michigan or Minnesota, it doesn't matter. We're near water and near Canada. And right then there was only me, the mom, to deal with and pay for the glowing angel on the treetop, whose flossy halo had already slipped. There was also the skateboard with the fire-eyed skull, the raveling hem of the expensive knee-length sweater, my Cooper ball glove, the boa constrictor.

The snake, at least, I hadn't bought. My son had brought it home in a garbage bag. Delvin had fed the thing, I didn't want to know what. Now the quietly patterned creature lay calm in a digestive torpor. It hadn't moved for hours, though I thought I'd seen its tongue flick once. If you are bitten by a rabbit or touched by the tongue of a snake, it is somehow good, I remembered. Wisdom? Long life? We could hope. And Tania had fallen out of love with her cat when it pooped in her shoes. She'd been asking for a new pet, so there was that, too. I don't have any sort of wealth or fall-back money. I run the tribal newsletter—which means I write, edit, photograph, print, and mail the thing—not a high-paying job but a 24/7 one.

Compared to the aftershock of what I'd spent, the snake had hardly registered. In fact, as it was clearly the one thing Delvin wanted more than anything else and he'd brought it home on Christmas Eve, and it was free, the snake was pretty much a welcome addition. What was getting me now was what my brother Raf had said about it. Raf is a tribal police officer. I'd run into him this morning. As we'd walked out of the grocery store together, I told Raf that Delvin had brought a big snake home. Like all our family, Raf has narrow eyes with brushy lashes, so you can't really see into his eyes unless he wants you to. When he opened his eyes wide for a second, I knew there was something.

'Uh-oh. I was afraid of this,' I said, and then asked him if we should keep the snake or if it put us in danger because of wherever it came from. He looked around and then leaned over.

'No, those guys are dead,' he told me.

Since then, I have been sitting before the aquarium in the air of spent-out excitement, staring at the snake. Raf had refused to explain the dead guys comment, for which I raised hell. Which he handled with a shrug. Now I was meditating on the situation. Delvin came in and sat beside me.

'You're watching it,' he said.

'Meditating.'

'There's some turkey left.'

'That sounds okay.'

'I'm going to make turkey soup,' said Delvin, who is a good cook. 'We got some wild rice from Raf. I'll use the canned tomatoes. An onion.'

'I think we should smudge the house,' I said, 'because when I talked to Raf, he told me the former owners of this snake were dead. I just think we should remove, you know, any untoward energy.'

'Okay,' said Delvin.

'That's all?'

'It's a good idea.'

He was definitely uneasy, eyelids fluttering. He just turned nineteen and is gone a lot these days. He's taking computer courses at our tribal college.

'You got the snake from a drug house,' I said.

Delvin tipped his face down and looked hard through the glass at the motionless snake. Its pattern looked ever more complex. Sorrow lowered over us.

'Okay, I'm going to smudge the snake. I wish you'd tell me what's going on.'

Delvin picked off a bunch of sage leaves from the bundle I'd gathered and rolled the leaves into a ball. I put the ball in my abalone shell, lighted the sage. Smoke rose in fragrant ribbons.

'Open the window so the smoke alarm doesn't go off,' I said.

'We don't have a smoke alarm. That's at work, Mom.'

'I put one in because of the Christmas tree. So open the window.'

Tania came into the room and put her face down to the sage. She whirled the smoke around her plugged-in ears, smiled dreamily, glided back into her room.

'Does she know?'

Delvin and I set the shell on top of the snake's cage and fanned the smoke down through the screen on top.

'Know what?' said Delvin.

I didn't speak. I didn't have to.

'I don't think so,' he said in a smaller voice.

The sage was ashes. Delvin got a kettle of salted water going and I started to chop the onion. He took the carcass out and began to pluck off the turkey meat. As he cleaned the bones, he put them in a pan of water to make the broth.

'If you won't tell me,' I said after a while, 'I'm going to have to start asking questions.'

'It's not like I don't want to tell you. I'm just having trouble approaching, you know, the subject of what happened.'

'Just tell it.'

Delvin washed his hands and dried them on a towel. He stood beside me as I scraped the onion to the side of the board and started on the carrots.

'The way it happened,' he began, 'is that a year or so ago I got a call from Wade.'

'A lot of things start with a call from Wade.'

'Okay, I know. Anyways, a couple years ago, Wade tells me that there are these two people living on a farm up near Hoopdance who have this really beautiful collection of exotic animals. Like they have a Siberian tiger which they keep in a barn, and they have a few buffalo. They have a gazelle and some emus— that's a bird.'

'Sort of like an ostrich?'

'Without those plumey tails.'

'I usually hear everything. Why don't I know about this?'

'They were kind of secretive, I guess. And they came from L.A.'

'Was this a meth lab or something?' I try to keep my voice neutral.

'No. Not meth. But besides the precious animals, they did have miniature horses and a huge kennel full of all kinds of dogs. And inside, this beautiful pink and white bird with a curled feather right on top of its head. They had two green parrots.'

'Why?'

'It was her dream, this woman.' Delvin took a deep, distressed gulp of air and his voice faltered. 'This woman, she had a beautiful soul. You know, an ancient soul. What she had always wanted was a farm filled with original creatures. And her husband had gone along with this as it was near reservation land out in nowheresville and so they had these animals and were keeping them. She spent a lot of time taking care of them. He did other stuff.'

'I can't believe I never heard about it. I should know about it. Gosh, Delvin, I should write it up for the newsletter.'

I was just fishing for some truth from him.

'No, Mom! I'm telling you, this is strictly confidential. There's more to it.'

I wiped my hand on the calendar towel and we stood there looking at each other until Delvin ducked his head.

'Yeah, well. Raf would say they weren't real normal or anything. There was a baby.'

'Was?'

'Is! Is! She was there when Wade and me—'

'Wade and I.'

'Wade and I. Let me start this over. Okay now, relax, Mom. Sit down.'

'I am not going to sit down. Just say it.'

'Okay okay then. A couple days ago, Wade and I drove out there to see the animals because they had got to be friends with Wade, and with I, so we parked beside the house and went up to the front door and never noticed the back door was hanging open and the tiger had attacked the husband and wife and ate most of him and a little bit of her and then stayed in the house where it was warm. So we just walk right in there and see the tiger dozing on the couch, and on the rug there was the baby girl and the snake was wrapped all around her and it wasn't, no, Mom, it wasn't squeezing her or eating her or anything. This is a good snake. They must have fed it. It was just sort of keeping her wrapped up and the baby was way bored though. She cried when she saw us. Wade picked up the snake and put it in the garbage bag and I picked up the baby and we tiptoed out and the tiger was still asleep on the couch.'

I reached backward and held on to the refrigerator. Delvin kept talking, agitated, seeing all of this in his head. His eyes were tearing up. He gasped his words out.

'We took the baby, but Raf confiscated her. He called in the FBI. Then the agent and the backups got there and the whole place was cordoned off while they tranquilized the tiger and got the other animals rounded up and I really don't know exactly why you never heard about this thing so you could report it for the newsletter, but Raf advised me not to tell you.'

'Advised you?'

'Raf said he'd toss me in the slammer if I told you, right yet anyway.'

'So I should question Raf if I want to know anything else?'

Delvin nodded in relief. He sat down and slumped away from me in the puffy chair before the television where I usually collapse after work. He put his hands up around his ears and tried not to cry.

Maybe out of terror I was reverting to my interview style. I do reporting for the newsletter, but mainly I am busy selling ads, correcting type, scanning in pictures, cleaning up the subscription list. I really found the mental image of the tiger on the couch eyeing the snake-encircled child and my son entering and exiting the scene—a couple of days ago, no less—confounding and pretty much unspeakable. I did not have the urge to talk to Raf about it. But before I could get my thoughts together, Raf came to the door, knocked once, walked inside.

'Hey, sis'—he was at the door, still in his uniform—'just off work.'

'Get in the kitchen then.'

I made new coffee for him. Delvin disappeared. I shoved a small box across the table, open, one truffle still plump in its fluted paper.

'Have the last one.'

He took it. 'How much do you know about Delvin's activities, Carleen?'

'I guess I don't know shit.'

He put the truffle in his mouth. His eyes took on a mysterious gleam. For a moment, he said nothing. Then he swallowed, sighed, sipped his coffee.

'Good chocolate ball.'

'I got them from an offer . . .'

'Uh-oh, Carleen. You gotta watch your online shopping habit.'

Raf had bailed me out last Christmas. Now he looked around warily for signs of other spree buying. But although I'd bought expensive, I'd bought small—the phone upgrade, the sweater folded in tissue on Tania's bed, the ball glove, and the longboard, already scuffed—there were no more chocolates.

'What is Delvin into? Just tell me.'

'I don't think he knows what he's into,' said Raf. 'Wade could be another story. You have to tell me right now, sis, do you cross the border much these days? I hope to god you don't drive up to Canada so regularly that anyone could predict.'

'Of course I do. Everybody drives up there. Sometimes we go to ceremonies with my friends, you know, make a cloth offering or whatever.'

'Oh great,' said Raf, wiping his forehead over and over. 'My sister the born-again pagan.'

'It's our tribal religion, Raf. No weirder than Catholicism.'

'You're a heathen, Carleen.'

'But Raf, we can pray for each other, hedge our bets. Were those snake people moving drugs across?'

'Duh. But they didn't do it themselves. They got other people, from god knows where. Not Canadians anyway. All this worries me real bad. I mean, your car could have been used without you knowing it, stuff taped underneath the hubcaps, that kind of thing. They could have someone retrieve it while you were lost in your oneness with the Creator.'

'Delvin wouldn't do that to me. Wade either. Probably.'

'Have you checked the snake?'

'It seems okay. It's a snake. It just hangs out on its electric rock. I really don't want the snake here to tell you the truth, but I only had one Christmas present for Delvin.'

Raf went over to the aquarium and took off the lid. He turned the lights way up, reached down, and examined the snake, turning it over, gently running his hands all the way up and down its length.

'What are you looking for?'

'Stitches. Sometimes they'll introduce Ziploc bags of whatever they are moving into animals. This one seems okay though. Besides, the big exotics are pretty obvious.'

'How do they get the drugs out?'

'How do you think.'

'Oh. What about the baby. Where's she?' I said finally.

Raf looked at me. He stepped away from the aquarium and spoke with a sympathy that chilled me.

December 26

'Now hold my hand, sis.'

'Oh fuck, what?'

'That little girl is Delvin's daughter.'

After a while, I said, 'So what else don't I know?'

'Um,' said Raf, 'that she's coming to live with you?'

DELVIN CAME IN later, looking solemn, and as I wasn't in the mood to talk either, we sat and flipped through the papers related to an unscheduled court date. Like around the death of my father when I was young, and the leaving of Kenny, what was there to say? Of course, those things were catastrophic. This was just a baby. A baby is good. But the mother apparently a drug dealer was not good. And what, an old woman? No, ancient soul. White? What was I to think of my son's having had sex with a married woman who was later partially devoured? I tell you, things happen here you would not believe even in a newsletter. Yet, my job is usually dull.

Delvin started to say something and I lifted my hand.

'I don't want any details.'

'This isn't details. It's kind of an explanation.'

'That either.'

Delvin sat there with me for a short while only before he couldn't help himself. He punched some buttons on his phone and handed me his daughter's picture. She was sitting on a pile of gifts in front of a perfect lighted tree. There was a brilliant red-eyed bird on one side of her and a monkey dressed up in an elf costume on the other. This had been taken a few days ago; she had lots of dark hair and her gums showed a tiny tooth. I handed the phone back.

'What's that supposed to tell me? I had assumed she was cute.'

I got up. I went to the bathroom and turned on the tap. The truth was she looked just exactly like Delvin had looked as a baby and I knew I was going to cry. Also, his phone was a model way past Tania's or anything I could afford and I'd never seen it before.

I came out when I was done. Delvin was still sitting there staring into the screen of the phone. His hair was flopped over his forehead as he bent over the image. He studiously avoided looking at me. The rule is if I go into the bathroom and turn on the tap for a long time, I do not want anyone to refer to the fact I was crying.

'What really scares me,' I said, sitting down beside Delvin, 'is not the baby, scary as that is. Not the tiger.'

'Yeah.'

'Were you part of the business?'

'Yeah.'

'Are you still part of the business?'

His eyes filled. He stared hard at the picture.

'I need some money,' he whispered.

'How much?' I asked.

He named a sum. More than everything we owned, all together, including the fancy sweater, my hidden box of truffles, and our long-term-payment electronic stuff. It was more than if the snake had been full of an expensive drug and stitched up. It was more than I'd ever had and more than the house was worth. I could feel it then. I could feel the cloth offering blowing off in the wind and the other face of the Creator coming at me. I got up and went to the window. There was nothing. Just the drive down to the road, some pines, and the snow, skimming gracefully off the tops of the drifts.

'You owe this money to . . .'

'Mom, you know better than to ask.'

'What about telling Raf? He'll protect us.'

Delvin looked at me kind of cross-eyed and opened his mouth.

Then he dropped his head in his hands and pulled on his hair. He spoke in grief.

'Oh Mom, it's as if you believed things were the other way around. Like cops protect you and get the bad guys and aren't mixed up in this thing. It's Raf you should worry about, Mom. You should worry about your brother. It's too fucking late for your son.'

His words, the situation, his sad-sack statement made me furious.

'We're going to see about that!' I jumped up and started pacing. Yeah! I smacked my hand in my fist. Summers, I play women's softball. It's my outlet. Fast pitch. Now this whole thing had me hyped up and I wanted to play some ball. I grabbed my Christmas glove.

'We're going out to the gym,' I said to Delvin. 'You're catching. I'm gonna burn 'em at you, baby, and by the time my arm gives out we will have a plan.'

THE GYM WAS full of holiday overeaters in a trundle fest. The numbers of sad, determined, easily defeated New Year's resolutions would grow through January, hang on to February, and by March the college gym would again be empty. But for now, our people walked determinedly around and around the walking path in the upper tier. The balcony of hope and shame. This is a gym with sharps disposal units in the bathrooms so that people can safely take their insulin before exercising. I pitched straight down the basketball court sideline and Delvin caught every pitch, only giving an occasional wince. I pitched out of terror. I pitched out of anger. I pitched out of tenderness. I wasn't ready for a grandchild, and certainly not prepared for the thought of how she came to be. I wasn't ready for the vast wall of money. I'd seen enough TV shows to know how this plotline ended up. There wasn't exactly a low-interest payment plan. They used sickening means to kill off the stupid bozo who messed up the drug deal or lost the money. There was sometimes a snake involved, a skateboard, a child, guns of course. A cop relative. A newsletter editor. But never a fast-pitch-playing mother. Maybe I would take out a couple of thugs with my ghost ball.

'Who are we up against?' I asked when we took a break.

Delvin named a member of the tribal council and two others.

'So just exactly in what way did you mess this thing up?'

My lungs clenched painfully. I couldn't take a deep breath.

'What did you do?' I whispered.

We were looking each other full in the face. In these movies the young drug dealer was abusive and mean and foul. Never like Delvin, who had never said an unkind word to me in his life. The good kid, that was Delvin. The worst he'd done was roll his eyes and stalk away from me.

'What did you do?' I asked again. 'Did you fill the snakes up with bags of drugs? Did you sew them up?'

'No,' he said. 'Not the snakes. I was supposed to do something I just couldn't do. Later on, I walked the stuff across myself.'

It was like I'd taken a fast pitch in the gut. I went down on the floor, on my ass. After a while I let Delvin help me back onto my feet. I looked at him, his eyes blazing sad underneath his straight, handsome eyebrows. His mouth was a kid's mouth, still tender. More than anything, I had always been afraid he would get fed up with school and enlist. The army recruits heavy among Indians.

As we walked out of the gym, I said maybe he should join the army.

'They can get you there, too,' he said.

We looked around the parking lot, which was 90 percent pickup trucks loaded with options. The vehicle of choice. Most would be repossessed by March, too, like all the gym-goers' lost pounds. We got into my car and I said that it must be exactly this sort of dilemma that made people knock over banks because frankly that was the only thing that I could think of to raise the money. Delvin said, yes, him too. And then we were silent.

OUR BIGGEST NEARBY city is a bubble of complexity surrounded by dense pine forest and then bare open highways and fields with no-where to hide. We scouted on a warmish January afternoon, wearing dollar-store eyeglass frames and Vikings stocking caps and jackets. We drove home, still brainstorming. Our plan was to use cash bor-rowed from Raf to buy a clunker car we could abandon, and also a used snowmobile. I would walk into the bank and stick up the teller, get the money, drive off, and park the car in the Walmart park-ing lot. Delvin would snowcat over and hide in a clump of scrub pines, waiting. We planned to wear metal-band-type wigs and were talking about where we could get *Matrix*-style long leather coats as we drove home. We stopped the car and sat in the driveway, our adrenaline spent, as if we'd done all of this already. Then we walked in the side door and sat down at the kitchen table. I made coffee and we heated up cans of soup. Suddenly everything gave out in me. I put my head down on the table.

'How stupid is this,' said Delvin in a choked-up voice.

Tania walked in wearing an extremely tight striped T-shirt over another even tighter T-shirt that came down over her extremely tight jeans.

'What's with you guys?'

'Our minds are running to desperation,' I said. 'Come here, baby.' I sat up. Tania put her arm around my shoulders and balanced on my lap.

'You guys are acting weird,' she said. She had washed, rinsed, heat-straightened, shined up, and lightly sprayed her hair. She had thrown her Xmas sweater over the T-shirts. Already I noticed a dangly piece of yarn.

'Where are you going?' asked Delvin.

'What's it to you, snake guy?'

'Who are you going with?'

'Hey,' I said. 'It's just to the game. I'm giving her a ride.'

Delvin looked away.

As we drove to the basketball game, I explained to Tania that her brother was tense.

'You think?'

'He's in bad trouble, Tania. Probably he's worried his trouble's going to land on you.'

'I kind of know what he was up to, Mom. I mean not all of it. I know about the baby now. When do we get her?'

'Uh, this weekend.'

'Unreal,' said Tania. She laughed. 'I don't care! We get the baby!'

Slumping happily in her parka, she reached out and traced her name in breath on the car window. 'Don't worry,' she said as she jumped out. 'Avril's dad will drive me home. He's supertough. He won't let anyone get at me.'

I drove home wishing I had a cigarette, although I'd given up smoking ten years ago. When I got back, Delvin was gone. He'd left a note. 'Don't worry. Also sorry. Snake got out.' I whirled around. The top was off the aquarium, just enough so that it did not look like a person had taken the snake out. It looked like the snake had gotten hungry. I sure hadn't fed the thing. I walked through the house, picking up couch pillows. Waiting for it to drop on me. Sling a coil around my ankle. I thought it would have gone to the warmest place in the house, which was the bathroom. I opened the door very carefully, but it was not in there or in any of the cupboards or along the pipes. The house was so quiet, I heard the hum of blood in my veins.

December 26

Delvin. I stood in the middle of the living room and punched Raf's number into my phone. The temperature was dropping. The house had aluminum ductwork put in when Kenny was here, but I'd never been able to afford to hook the new ductwork up to a new furnace, which also I'd forgotten to purchase. The old boiler was cranky. And when it got really cold it sulked. I heard the snake slide through the ductwork in the ceiling.

'I'll be right over,' said Raf when I told him Delvin was gone. But when he came, we could find no sign of any struggle and no unusual tracks in the snow. We stood in the kitchen. I took a cigarette from Raf and smoked. It just made me dizzy. The wall clock shook as the snake slithered down behind it, between the studs.

'Social services is bringing the baby over tonight,' said Raf, eyeing the wall clock. 'There's been an emergency.'

'Emergency?' I started crying. The snake twitched in the floor.

'Did you hear that?'

'Yeah.' But he didn't mean the snake. 'I think that's social services driving up right now,' he said.

So I got the baby. And she was a very dear little baby with a jubilant attitude and a topknot. Given the furnace situation, I kept her in her snowsuit. The social services people drove off. There was a hissing sound of old Sheetrock dust sifting through the walls. The snake was on the move again. Tania came home and we all kept our coats on. The temperature was still going down.

'They warned us at the game, Mom. Sub-subzero. Minus thirties. I'm sleeping in your bed.'

'Great. I'll put the little electric heater in the room. The baby can sleep between us.'

'We gotta stick together,' said Tania. 'That snake is beginning to creep me out.'

'It's just catching mice,' I said.

'We don't have mice.'

I left the water running just a trickle in all of the sinks and opened the cupboards so the pipes would not freeze. From time to time, the furnace pumped out a thread of lukewarm air. I put our other heater in the kitchen. At least we had our electric. We searched every inch of the bedroom. The snake had stopped making noise. I didn't like that. We put all of the cellophane bags we could find on the floor. The room looked like a junk food orgy, but we thought the snake would crackle if it slithered across. We got in bed with double parkas, wool beanies, extra socks. We put the baby between us in her snowsuit and piled all the blankets we could find on top of us. I stayed awake most of the night, waiting for the bags to crinkle, my brain racing. Delvin. And the snake. I tried to calm myself down with deep breathing. But pictures came. It could slither up and eat the baby. It could strangle Tania. Could I wrestle it to death? Stab it with the jackknife beneath my pillow? Finally, I dropped off. We slept warm, but when we woke there was frost on the blankets from our breath. Our furnace just couldn't pump out enough heat.

Tribal offices shut down. Most everyone stayed home. The milk was frozen solid in the fridge. I could have bowled a strike with the head of lettuce. I unpeeled the carton from the milk and warmed the block of milk on the gas stove. Trickling the water overnight had saved the pipes. I made oatmeal and we took our bowls back to bed. Tania brought our laptop in and we stayed in the blankets all morning, playing with the baby. She had a little punk squirt of hair, her eyes were deep brown, and she squeezed them shut when she gurgled and smiled. Every so often I got weak all over and couldn't breathe. I mumbled something about Delvin going off with Raf, and Tania pretended to believe me. By noon, the floor was warm enough to walk on without our snow boots and we went out to the living room. The baby nestled into a sleeping bag and fell asleep.

December 26

'Look,' called Tania. 'The snake's back.'

It had returned to the cage and its warm rock. There was a bulge in its middle. I went over to the aquarium and decided to top the cover with a big board and a heavy rock. The snake was shaped funny.

'Is that a wad of mice? Did you feed it mice?'

'Of course not.'

'Were there mice in the walls? Did it get some mice?'

'I don't know,' said Tania, thoughtful.

We stared at the thing.

After a while she said, 'Hey, Mom, have you seen the cat?'

IT TOOK ME most of the day to track down Kenny Thunder. He was playing down in Tucson at some Indigenous fest, with his band and his usual female lead singer—he would be having an affair with her. She would leave when she got sick of him. The band was always breaking up and reconstituting over the repeated singer/Kenny phenomenon. I kept tabs on him through his sister, though she usually had only the second-to-latest girlfriend's name and number. Kenny often changed his own number after a breakup. I went through several women who sounded pissed off until I told them Kenny's son was missing. When I finally talked to Kenny, he turned out, or so he said, to be sober and between women. He would take the next flight to the city and rent a car. Sometimes Kenny got big waves of feeling for his family. Last summer, he'd shown up with lavish gifts and he'd cried over Tania's long legs and Delvin's new biceps. He started some house-improvement projects. Then he vanished again. Nevertheless, now, with Kenny on the way, I felt like something was getting done.

Never mind that he was good at taking charge and making sure nothing happened.

Maybe that was just it. Nothing bad usually happened around Kenny. He lived by the rule that anything that anybody did, especially himself, was basically okay. There were no bad intentions. He did not hold grudges. He himself never meant any harm, no matter how much he hurt people. He really did count intentions as actions and his were always good, so how could anybody harm him? Even so, the revenges that his tribal girlfriends took on him were legendary.

Sheila from Green Bay had microwaved his precious hair products until they fused with their plastic containers, then she'd hot-wired his blow-dryer to shock him. Angela had drowned his guitar in the bathtub, left it on the radiator to warp, sliced up his shirts. Wannette had collected a jar of bedbugs and let them loose in his apartment. Later, she sent a note. Randi was a Red Laker and her revenge topped them all. She got him stinking drunk and fake-seduced him, then superglued him into his bedsheets, superglued his penis to her discarded panty hose and his precious skinny ponytail to his pillow. She'd also put his new guitar and his fabulously expensive elk-hide cowboy boots into a wood chipper that she'd bought and charged to him.

All of these acts of vengeance were no more to Kenny than funny stories. He even told them to his new girlfriends, who one-upped their predecessors when inevitably they caught him cheating. As angry as he made people, though, he had no real enemies. His charm wasn't superficial, he genuinely liked people and was generous. He paid child support even when he had no bookings. He remembered our birthdays with birthday cards from the road. He was tender, supportive, loving with the children when he was here. He'd never had other children, never wanted to. He'd even had a vasectomy and maintained that he was proud of shooting blanks. All in all, the worst thing about Kenny as an ex-husband, besides his womanizing, was first his absence, and then that I was still self-disgustedly one-sixteenth in love with him. Or he could get to me. Same thing.

However, this was a whole other situation.

I had promised myself years ago that I'd stop putting on lipstick or eye makeup, stop trying to look good, when Kenny was about to show up. This was the first time I didn't catch myself at it. I was terrified, or beyond terrified, probably. Tania let Kenny in and I woke from a crashing nap to feel my hand in his warm palm. I sat up, he held me tight, and let me cry. With my head against his chest, I noticed he had stopped working out—his pecs were soft and droopy. He was telling the truth about being between women. His arms were plush and bearlike.

'Ah ma petite, ma honey, go ahead and cry. We'll find our boy, don't you worry none. What the Holy Lord?'

Tania had walked in with the torpid snake draped around her.

'Please put the snake back, sweetheart,' I said calmly.

'Okay, Mom. I'm sorry. I just wanted to impress Dad.'

'I'm for sure impressed,' said Kenny.

'It belongs to Delvin,' I said.

Tania's voice trembled and she began to stroke the mottled length of muscle. It twisted slowly from her arms as she brought it back to the aquarium. Kenny cleared his throat several times before he could speak.

'That's a big old snake, ennit,' he said at last.

Then the baby crept from the quilt I was under and Kenny stared at her and said, 'Holy Jesus, a baby. Come on over here, little honeybud.'

He gave me a look of respect and said, 'You still got it, girl.'

'She's Delvin's baby.'

'Eyyy, that's . . . ah, real nice.'

He cuddled her and said, 'We'll find your papa. Don't you worry none.' And I almost believed him.

The next morning, on the way to the kitchen, I noticed something missing. After my second cup of coffee, I realized it was the aquarium. I didn't ask about it, just left that to Tania.

'We're not sleepin' with no snake in the house,' Kenny said to her in an earnest voice.

'Where'd you put it?' she asked.

'I put it in the garage. To hibernate.'

Tania marched out there and came back in.

'It's frozen solid.'

'So you *think*, my sugar. Come here and let me cook up some instant oatmeal. Strawberries 'n Cream?'

She nodded in a distracted way.

'Snakes don't hibernate,' she said in a hurt voice. She wasn't really hurt. We still hadn't seen the cat.

'Hey, I'm sorry about the snake too,' I said. 'But we have a baby here now.'

Tania's eyes went big and round.

'Delvin said he's a good snake.'

'Snakes don't have morals,' I said.

'Some do,' said Kenny, meaning himself I think.

I LOOKED AT him suspiciously, and he made a sign that we'd talk later. That afternoon, standing in the driveway, he wanted to discuss his moral whatever.

'I'm closing shop,' he promised.

'Closing shop as in shooting blanks? Or no more extra women?'

'That last thing.'

I looked at him carefully and said, 'You always blink when you lie.'

He tried not to blink but his eyes seemed to strain and he shook his head. 'Aw hell. Why would you believe me anyways. I long for you, Carleen.'

December 26

'It's not that I don't believe you in this minute. But you've closed shop before, Kenny, and this isn't the time or place.'

'So true, ma lovergirl. Well, anyway, I'm going out now. Gonna hit the roads and look for our boy. Gonna go up the border. Talk to people.'

'Bring him back,' I said.

Kenny put his arms around me and it felt good, as long as I turned off all common sense.

LATER ON STILL, I got a call from Kenny. He said he had to stay up there and follow up with some musicians. The way he said it felt like musicians were code for something else, and I almost said, 'Be careful.' Then again, maybe he was visiting an old ex-lead singer. So I said that I'd let Tania know. In case he had actually developed scruples, I let warmth creep into my voice. I got the week's edition out, somehow, with the baby in a playpen made of liquor store boxes stuffed with old issues. Working on the newsletter soaked up some panic, although my proofreading wasn't perfect and my brain kept running scenarios. If Delvin was kidnapped. Dumped from a car. Lying in a snowy ditch. The problem was that none of my fantasies was as outlandish as what had in fact already happened. What was happening now could be outlandish beyond all description.

I BROUGHT THE baby to a spiritual person, along with Tania, to get traditional names. Hoping they would be protected by those names. We took drives to look for Delvin, went up past the border and all around the roads and ditches, then back. I'd blinked away thoughts of him lying dead in the pines or in a frozen field. Then at home, when I tried to sleep, I could see those fields so clearly, the frosted stubble and icy waves of snow blown hard as glass.

At last, after weeks had passed, Delvin showed up in the yard while I was chipping ice. I turned around and there he was, shabby and thin. Smote by his sudden presence, I went down on my knees. He crouched before me and put his hand on my shoulder. His baby was playing in the yard, a snowsuited bundle, and she wouldn't go to him. Finally, his baby let him pick her up and we walked back into the house. I followed him into the kitchen, dizzy, and sat down at the table with the baby on my lap, to hide my shaky legs.

'What. Where. Tell me.'

'I'll tell you later, Mom.'

'Tell me now.'

'Okay. It was okay. I did the job I had to do. It's done.'

'What was it?'

'No, later.'

'Now.'

'Dogs.'

'What dogs?'

'Remember how I told you they had a kennel of dogs? They were all medium-sized brown dogs, just regular dogs, fluffy hair. I kept those dogs clean, all nice and brushed. That's how I got involved in the first place. Me and Wade took care of the dogs.'

I didn't remember, but I nodded.

'They got those dogs from dog pounds, Mom. Those were, you know, extra dogs. Dogs that society was going to put to death. But every one of those dogs had a personality.'

I looked at him sharply. Tears started running along the sides of his face, the way he'd cried as a kid.

'And papers. Those dogs had papers. Vet papers. To say they were all up-to-date on shots and so forth. All they needed to go across the border was those papers. And those two, you know, they were a nice-looking couple, would travel with a couple of dogs. The dogs sleeping in back because of sleeping pills. They have already put the dog into sedation, cut the dog open, and sewed in plastic tubes of whatever, drugs and all. Sometimes they would use the same dog a couple or three times. After a while, it would die. I'm sorry, Mom.'

'Okay, I get it. Raf told me about the snake thing.'

'There's more room inside of dogs and they're, I guess, cheap. I'm sorry I left you with the snake.'

'It froze.'

'You want to know about Dad, don't you.'

I felt the blow like I was slugged in the heart.

'Tell me.'

When he didn't answer, I had my answer. We sat there. I put a handful of Cheerios on the table and Delvin's baby picked up each one with a critical air, then put it carefully into her mouth. I was too stricken to be sad, too tired to be tired, too angry to be angry, and knew that right here was the beginning of grief. Delvin said, 'Mom, I am out. Done. I am not going back. I promise you that.'

'You're not going back for your dad. That's for the FBI or DEA or RCMP or some agency to handle. You're not going, no, no, no.'

'Of course not, Mom.'

His eyelids fluttered.

'You always do that when you lie,' I said.

We stared at each other and I saw that frozen field.

THE FERAL TROUBADOUR

Let the wind have its way, then the earth that invades as dust and then the dead foaming up in gray rolls underneath the couch.

Leave the dishes. Let the celery rot in the bottom drawer of the refrigerator.

your heart, that place you don't even think of cleaning out. That closet stuffed with savage mementos. Don't sort the paper clips from screws from saved baby teeth.

Talk to them. Tell them they are welcome.

pink will gr those in th Accept of life

don't read thing ex t de trays the between experience. un on aters l drich

The bathroom in my apartment is a special project—cheap black and white linoleum tiles for the floor and up along the bathtub wall. Each white tile bears a poem copied out by hand, by me, using a permanent marker. Polyvinyl gloss preserves my best cursive. This is so that I can continue my father's schoolteacher habit of memorizing poems. My landlord is okay with it — because his plan is to tear down the house, I suspect. I'm between jobs, between everything. This place is cheap and I get a further cut for looking after things when my landlord is out of town. He mostly lives in Palm Springs.

My apartment is the third floor, a converted attic. I have no shower, only a claw-foot bathtub, which didn't seem very manly when I first moved in. Now I love lolling in the water, memorizing a line or two. Not long ago, I learned how difficult my project was to clean. Some of the poems are short, like 'Luck,' by Langston Hughes, which has survived the cat. Robert Pinsky's 'Antique' nearly disappeared under grubby paw prints.

As I scrub away at *this cold sunlight falling on this warm earth*, I can't help thinking about how many feral cats I have tried to tame. I'm not a cat guy, but I have never been able to leave one to its misery or doom. I have captured and often tamed or found a new home for tattered felines. With false joviality, I have posted online photos, described their cattish qualities with wit and care, hoping that some cat lover might take pity and keep that cat forever indoors, babying it tenderly, so that it kills no birds. I subscribe to a world that includes the indigo bunting.

I am also a bumbling poet. Scrubbing away, I realize that I've haplessly written a poor imitation of Louise Glück's elegant and supple lines. I am a sparrow trying to imitate an indigo bunting. But I don't mind. I have modest requirements, and not all poets have to be published. I waste no trees.

A few weeks ago, the yard of this apartment house I share was haunted by an emissary of the divine. The indigo bunting, possessed of blue feathers the supernatural color of the Virgin's cloak, took up temporary lodgings in the tasseled birches. When the western light slanted down its wings glowed, it was Rilke's torso of Apollo. *You must change your life*. A poem written on my bathroom floor on the tile beside the digital scale.

All of this poetry is now marked by the penetrating reek of cat. I am using a citric-acid-based cleaner that singes my hands. It will leave my poetry floor smelling like an orange grove. Such is my hope.

MY STORY, HOWEVER, the one I am telling here, makes no sense unless I also tell the story of how I lay in wait six days ago, in the green depth of summer, after the visit from the indigo bunting. I was hoping that a cat would risk everything for a sardine. One always drinks while trapping a feral cat. And so I was. As I sat on my back step, I was tuned for the snap of the live trap's metal plate that would mean the starved, slinky, green-gray and gold-eyed tabby, still a rangy kitten, thus beaten up by older cats, had gone for the bait.

MY APARTMENT HOUSE lies on a pedestrian thoroughfare that leads to a secluded lake beach that was once notorious for drugs, crime, nudity, and sordid, dangerous fun. Although the neighborhood association has made the beach more wholesome, the site of yoga and logrolling, there are still hot summer days when a phalanx of naked bicyclists will stream past this place on their way to take a dip. A person luridly drunk or tripping will sometimes curl up beneath a tree on the boulevard. There might even be a passing troubadour.

That night, as I sipped and waited for the cat in the green gloom, I heard the tones of a strummed guitar. The song, which I did not recognize, abruptly stopped in front of the house. The other tenants were gone. My downstairs neighbor, whom I've dated, whose room faces the street on which the singer moaned, was on vacation. Could the singer be another fellow trying to win her? He struck a mournful chord. Simultaneous with the chord, the trap clashed shut. I was caught between impulses. Should I check the trap first or tell the troubadour to fuck off? And what was this new song he was beginning in a lower, troubling, key? Oh no, it was that Springsteen song 'I'm on Fire.' It is an undeniably sexy song. But of course, an actual strange man serenading my adorable neighbor's window with this song was disturbing. The drink sloshed in my cup as I lurched forth to confront the singer moaning *ohhhohhhohhh I'm on fire.*

There is a streetlamp in front of my house. I reared out of the gloom.

'Good evening.'

The guitar player, in that part of the song mimicking the sound of a lonesome freight train whistle, startled, *oooo-ack*, nearly dropping his guitar and cutting short the sound of bleak desire. He clutched his heart, panted. His springy brown hair, middle parted, stuck out on each side of his face like short wings. His eyes were small, his nose and chin round, his body thick and strong. I could see, instantly, that I'd have trouble taking him. The music man wore a floppy checked shirt, cargo shorts, sandals, was probably in his midthirties, and underemployed, like me. I asked him if he was serenading anybody in particular.

'Not really,' he gulped, still catching his breath. 'I just stopped here because it didn't look like anybody was home.'

'Well, I'm home,' I said. 'And I wouldn't mind if you were to play a different song. Coming back from the beach?'

'Yeah. The scene has changed.'

'So it has. But I'd sit here on my front steps and listen if you played something else.'

He played 'Sea of Heartbreak.' Sang off-key.

'I sense a certain theme,' I said when he'd finished.

'I suppose it's obvious. She's gone, gone, gone. Literally, leaving on a jet plane.'

'Don't play that song,' I said, with a pang.

I could tell he meant to and he wanted to. He was silent, then he spoke.

'May I come in?' he asked. 'Just to use the john?'

I didn't answer, stepped down onto the sidewalk and then past him into the streetlamp glow. There were a couple of people at the end of the street.

'No,' I said. 'Move on.'

'I really have to relieve myself, brohhhhh.'

He shouldered his guitar, unzipped his cargo shorts, and began the process of taking a leak on the tattered lawn. The people had turned the corner and there was nobody else in the street. His fake politesse while pissing enraged me, but I didn't care to challenge him. Finally, he gave a little shake, turned, and walked away. Before he reached the end of the next street, he began singing 'Leaving on a Jet Plane.'

I stood alone. It had only been one date, but I missed her. And I still had to deal with the feral cat in its wire cage.

The Feral Troubadour

—————

THAT NIGHT, SLEEP would not give me an out. I had that feeling that sometimes comes over me. The sense that I have failed to be a mature, or at least normal, person. I couldn't argue myself out of it. A possible rival had pissed on my lawn before my eyes, and there was now a feral cat living in my bathroom. I thought about how the charmed awkwardness of my youth has now hardened to a different sort of awkwardness entirely. I feel uncouth. It seems I've vanished from honorable view and am ghosting along here in my cluttered rooms, mistaking my daily putters and nightly soul wander for actual happiness. I was awake in the dark for about an hour before, as always, this discomfort and sorrow fell away from me and a sense of relief, of intrigue, of having found the secret so many people yearn for, crept up on me.

No, I was fine. More than fine. Happy. I had just enough money to get me to my next job. I was free. And I had a love interest who had said, before leaving, *Let's keep in close touch*. I was now writing a poem with the title 'In Close Touch.' However, she only texted every few days when she and her girlfriends went into town. They were camping out of cell range.

Although from time to time the cat in my poetry bathroom thumped, jolting the aluminum heating panels, and although it threw itself around the room, sending plastic bottles of soap and shampoo crashing to the floor, there was nothing more wrong with me than most. Tomorrow would dawn. I would search out people who tamed feral cats. I would consult them. I would bring this cat, a female, to a vet for her operation and her shots. This, I could do. Then I would find a saint. Someone would take this cat from my poetry bathroom. I would again be free to memorize or not memorize, without the poor cat lurching toward the windows, climbing the sink, launching herself from the toilet to the rim of the tub, eyeing me with outright panic or the veiled eyes of contempt.

FOR A COUPLE of days, I kept the cat in my bathroom, fan operating at all times. Because the door latch was broken, I rigged up a mechanism to keep it from swinging open. Two lanyards, one bearing a school security badge, the other an entry pass to Seth's Bar Mitzvah 2005, plus a thirty-pound kettlebell, composed the lock. I looped the lanyard to the doorknob, attached the second lanyard to the kettlebell, tied them together. I could squeeze into the cat-taming bathroom by lifting the kettlebell and slipping through the doorway. The cat knew and tried to charge me, feinting at my feet, but I was always ready. Once in, I wore a dust mask, because the cat was rife with cat dust. Within just forty-eight hours of being fed, she fluffed out, and although she froze whenever I stepped near, she was beginning to accept me. If I moved too quickly, though, she would literally climb the wall. She leaped up picture frames and wall hooks, pulling down or smashing whatever was smashable. Every time I went in, there was something to throw out, something I hadn't noticed was even in the bathroom. It was one way of decluttering.

I put out some online pleas and was desperate enough to leave my phone number. I took the advice of a feral cat tamer on a YouTube channel. She was British, young, and she wore black swoops of eyeliner that made her catlike. Her voice was purring and seductive. Every time I went into the cat's presence, I was supposed to do something good so that the cat would associate me with good things. So I did. I left food, scooped litter, refilled water, and eventually managed to give the cat a few strokes.

The Feral Troubadour

Whenever I put my hand out to touch the cat, I hummed a soothing song. I didn't want to meet the cat's eyes, but I felt hers, flat yellow with hate, tracking my hand. I also felt her body turn to cement. Yes, when I touched her, the cat's flesh grew cold and dense. She became an inert statue and there was nothing I could do to bring back the soft magic of her intrinsic catness. I tried to shake off a sense of being judged as a man. It had only been a few days, but unless you've kept a feral cat in your bathroom you can't imagine how it breaks you down.

IT WAS LATE evening and there were voices outside the front of the house. I went outside and there he was, on the lawn, right where he had pissed. Only this time there were two police officers with him. One was shining a flashlight on some sort of document. I stepped out the door.

'May I help you?'

'Yes, yes, you may help!' cried the troubadour.

The officers turned toward me. One was a beautiful, formidable woman.

'We're looking for someone in the area who's been breaking into people's houses. There was a house broken into a few nights ago. People also heard a guy singing and playing a guitar.'

'Well, if they heard the playing it would prove I'm not the guy,' the troubadour argued. 'Because how could I break into a house at the same time that I was playing a guitar?'

'I don't know,' said the woman officer. 'Maybe you played as you walked away with a pocket full of stolen jewelry and a guitar case with two laptops inside slung across your shoulder.'

The two officers and the musician looked at me.

'Tell them I was here,' said the guitar player, 'and that I wasn't breaking into your house. Oh, and didn't have a guitar case.'

At that moment, had I not still been angry that he'd pissed on my lawn, I might have considered the fact that he could have been singing in order to draw out anybody who was home. Maybe in fact he had been checking out the apartment house as he train-whistled. But instead of mentioning that theory, I just became vindictive.

'I'm not sure I saw this guy,' I said.

The officers suddenly seemed bigger, and the troubadour much smaller, and I seemed bigger too, perched on my front steps, looking down at them.

'Why don't you step into the light?' I said to the young man. I was ashamed of the tone of my voice. I realized now that I could get this jerk into a lot of trouble. I might have somewhat hated him, but I didn't know if I wanted him to be in all that much trouble. Under the streetlight the troubadour's winglike hair drooped. He slumped. He seemed a beaten man. He didn't look like he had the strength or determination to break and enter.

'What day and time did the break-in occur?' I asked.

'Eight p.m. Five nights ago.'

I thought about it. Counted back. I wasn't sure, but decided on mercy.

'Five nights ago, right around that time, this fellow was singing "Sea of Heartbreak" and pissing on the lawn. I don't really want to give him an alibi, but it's pretty clear he couldn't have been breaking into another house at that time.'

'All right. You say he was relieving himself here?'

The woman said this with a hint of sarcasm.

'He pissed, but he was discreet,' I said, knowing how pissy I myself sounded but unable to walk it back. 'You really behaved very badly,' I said to the guitar player. 'It was uncalled-for.'

The Feral Troubadour

'You are right. I am so sorry.'

It was like we were uttering lines from a high school play.

'Go your own way,' I said.

'Walk on,' said the male officer.

'Before I leave,' the troubadour said, 'any requests?'

'"Leaving on a Jet Plane,"' said the woman officer.

The troubadour raised his eyebrows at me. I lowered my eyebrows at him. He began to play as he walked down the street. The cat yodeled in the attic.

I WENT BACK into the house. My cell phone started buzzing. I picked it up, my heart leaping, but I didn't recognize the name.

'I am returning your call about the cat,' said a pleasant woman's voice. This was the second-best call I could have received.

'Can it be?'

'Yes, I would like to keep a feral cat in my house. It would be a privilege to tame this creature and I promise, as you ask, to make it an indoor cat.'

'You are the best human being in the whole world,' I said. Then tears closed my throat. I couldn't speak. That another human was capable of providing me this deliverance overpowered me.

AS THE STRONG young man with the wilted hairdo walks off playing the song made famous by Peter, Paul, and Mary, he thinks, What fools. And more fool he! The weenie who vouched for me even though I pissed quite openly on his lawn. He must have seen my impressive wanger and compared it to his pinkydoodle. So here I am. Free to sing my favorite song before I go back to rob him. For of course he was off by a whole day and night. Completely off his head, probably. There will be something in that house to steal. I'll do my trick. Use the ladder I see across the alley, left hanging on the outside of his garage. Scale high as I can. They never lock those windows.

I SLEEP HARD, downstairs on the couch in the shared living room. I couldn't stand the upstairs cat reek. I wake to the repeated chiming of the entry doorbell. It is very early morning, and the same two police officers as before, looking tired, probably at the end of their shifts, are at the front door. I open the door to speak to them. There is apparently a man screaming on the roof. At first I am too confused with sleep to register that the faint but ghastly shrieks, prolonged wavering yowls, are coming from my own upstairs apartment.

'May we come in?'

'I should say so!'

We walk up the stairs, the two holding me back and climbing protectively ahead of me. I'm touched by this and explain to them the mechanism of the kettlebell locking system attached to the door-knob. They nod as if they are familiar with my setup, then carefully pull the weight back to open the door. There is a storm of sound in there. The officers enter cautiously, though they do not draw their weapons. The air reeks of cat, but not as badly as in the beginning, when I did not run the fan. At the window, which can immediately be seen from the open door, the contorted face of the troubadour looms, his desperation intense. The poor cat has plastered herself to the wall, behind the toilet, tail a bottle brush, eyes round and freak-ish. Horribly, at the windowsill, fingers caught in the sash have gone deep purple. Now things become really challenging. For if the win-dow is opened, the man may fall off the ladder. If indeed he is even on a ladder and not held there by his fingers. The officers make some quick phone and radio calls. As the uniformed woman speaks to the

dispatcher and waits for an answer, her eyes wander across the poetry walls. Her lips move gently and she nods.

In what seems a very short amount of time, there are sirens. A
fire truck is positioned so the man can be hooked to a firefighter
who is also hooked to a ladder. The window is carefully opened and
the man is safely detached from the house. In terror, the cat darts
into another room. Or at least I hope she does. If the cat gets out of
my apartment, I'll never catch her. She'll never fall for that sardine
trick again.

The morning passes. All the excitement has moved on. The
woman who would like a feral cat in her house comes to the front
door. She is dressed in jeans and a plain gray sweatshirt. There is
something indescribably kind about her, and I would do anything for
her. Anything but keep this cat.

'The cat slipped into my bedroom,' I say. 'She's behind a chest of
drawers.'

From her bag, the woman takes a pair of leather gloves that reach
to her elbows. She also has a cat carrier.

'No problem at all,' she says. 'I can't wait to meet the cat.'

On her knees, wearing the gloves, she peers behind the dresser.
Then she backs away, arranges the carrier near her heels, and asks me
for a flashlight. I have one handy. She leans forward, shines the light
in the cat's eyes, and swiftly reaches around the head, grabs the cat
by the nape of its neck the way a mother carries its kitten, and lowers
it, flailing and hissing, into the carrier.

'We're gonna be best friends, aren't we,' she says into the little grate
on top of the carrier. The cat screams at her. 'Now say goodbye!'

I look down through the shiny metal wires. The cat stares fixedly
at me, eyes of lemon gold shrouded and filled with an unreadable ex-
pression somehow like my own eyes. We are alike. Our needy bodies,
our thrumming hearts.

I go up to the cat bathroom to assess the damage, but there is no damage. Everything is filthy, broken, or in disarray, but there is no damage. I begin the process of washing and cleaning, tenderly wiping around the text of each poem. I feel as close to normal as I've ever felt. I scrub the floor and work until my fingers turn purple, like the troubadour's fingers, which makes me wonder about him enough, by the next morning, to call the police officer, who had given me her number. She answers, I ask, and she tells me that she will inquire for me at the hospital. Later, she calls back to tell me that his guitar-strumming fingers were entirely saved and that he was probably the same thief they were looking for when they questioned him the other night. She says they found out what happened when he tried to enter the upstairs bathroom.

'He said that he was attacked by a cat. He was trying to get back out the window when the cat slammed the sash down on his fingers.'

'But the cat was terrified. And how would it slam down a window?'

'He says it jumped on top of the sash.'

'Of course,' I say, 'it was always trying to climb up the window. It could have caused the window to slam shut. But still, I'm surprised it would attack him.'

'I agree. It isn't like a cat,' the officer says.

Except this cat, I think, and cannot wait to tell the kind adoptive woman of her new cat's heroism. I also ask the officer if she would possibly like to meet me for a drink, and she doesn't hang up.

'I'll think about it,' she answers. 'You're cute.'

In hope, I take the lanyard off the kettlebell and put the weight where I'll either start lifting it or pretend I don't see it.

THAT NIGHT, I fall asleep knowing there is always a chance I will wake in the night certain I am an outcast, outside the common run of humanity, an impostor by light of day. There is still no text from my camping neighbor, but I feel better for having been called cute by a beautiful woman in a uniform. Still, I'm pretty sure I will fall into that well of embarrassment sometime or another, again. And I wonder. Can it be that all of us upon waking sometimes feel malformed or broken, foolish, as we huddle in our nests all over the earth? Perhaps, I think, this pit of shame without perspective is the true human connection. Perhaps this sharing of soul dregs is what makes it possible to write a poem. My heart is full of this thought but I end up writing about the kind woman who loves cats. She has called to tell me that the cat was tamed instantly by seeing another cat in her lap, eating cat treats. Perhaps this will spare the indigo bunting, but I'd also be happy with a sparrow. The most I can probably aspire to is to be counted among the people who care for the small, the ordinary, the overlooked creatures of the earth. Because I am one, and it appears that I am contented with a glance from a pretty woman and the poetry on a clean bathroom floor.

BIG CAT

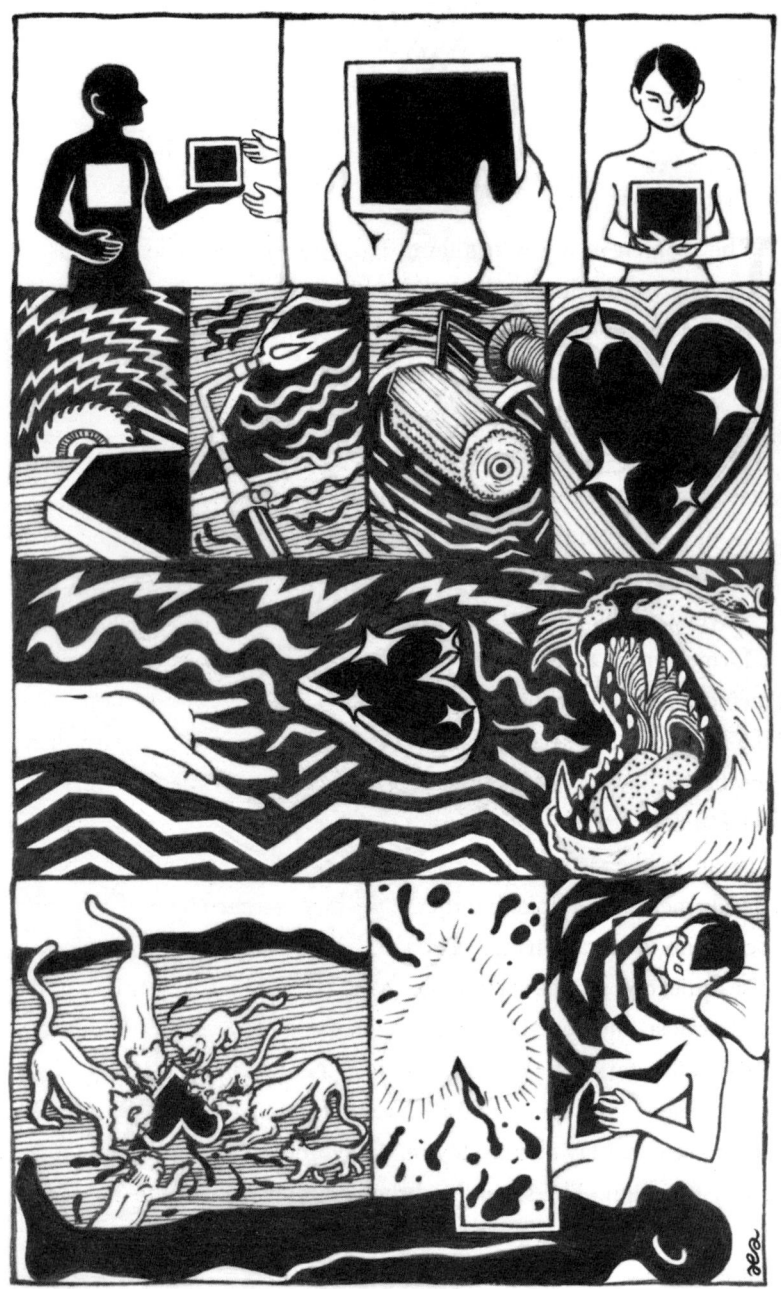

The women in my wife's family all snored, and when we visited every winter during the holidays I got no sleep. Elida's three sisters and their bombproof husbands loved to gather at her parents' house in Golden Valley, an inner-ring suburb of Minneapolis. The house was less than twenty years old, but the sly tricks of the contractor were evident in every sagging sill, skewed jamb, cracked plaster wall, tilted handrail, and, most significantly, in the general lack of insulation that caused the outer walls to ice up and the inside to resound.

Every night the sounds were different. Helplessly cognizant, I formed mental scenarios while drifting in and out of sleep. One memorable night, I tossed and turned in a metalworking shop. From the far end of the second-floor hallway came the powerful rip of my mother-in-law's rough-cut saw. From below, on the living room's foldout couches, the intermittent thrum of welders' torches—a wild hissing as the sisters' noses sparked and soldered invisible objects. Beside me, Elida's finishing touch: the high-pitched burr of a polisher perfecting a metal surface. Elida was slight, and she dressed in precise, quiet colors. She sat with her hands folded, wore clear nail polish and almost undetectable makeup. You would never have imagined that such a stark little person could produce such sounds.

Ambien, earplugs, two pillows on my head—nothing could shut the noise out. I lay awake stewing, even though I knew I should feel sorry for them. The sisters and their mother had visited sleep clinics, endured surgery, blown their CPAPs off their faces, tried every nose strip and homoeopathic remedy that existed. It wasn't that they liked to snore but that they were incurable. I think they took comfort in solidarity though. Elida admitted that she loved sleeping in that noisy house, and sometimes they snored in unison—which was terrifying.

One subzero vacation morning, my daughter, Valery, ran her finger across the frost-furred downstairs living room wall and asked, 'What is this, Daddy?'

'Snores,' I said, blue with tiredness. 'All of the snores from last night have stuck to the walls.'

Later, after her mother and I had divorced, Valery wistfully recalled that moment as the first time she'd realized how alive with sound the night was—and that all the noise emanated from the women in the family. Later still, she asked her mother at what age she'd begun to snore, and asked me if that was the reason we'd split up. Valery was worried for her own future. I assured her that snoring had had nothing to do with the divorce, which was amicable, but also unavoidably painful. I laughed and hugged Valery. I even told her that I had adored her mother's snores. I had never adored them, but I had adored Elida, almost to the point of madness, from the first time we met.

We found each other in Hollywood, as Minnesotan expatriates always do, common sense driving them together—though to leave the Land of 10,000 Lakes for a thirsty city built on a desert may speak of some interior flaw. For Elida, it was the compulsive lure of film editing. In my case, the shame of acting. Although I auditioned endlessly and always worked, my parts generally lasted between six and twelve seconds. I rarely had a line. But I had Elida, her intensely focused green stare, her Nordic pallor, even after years of sunlight, her slender, gliding walk, and the dark swerve of her severe haircut. She was mine.

Big Cat

––––––––

WHEN VALERY TURNED fourteen, I was cast in a supporting role that got a lot of attention. It could have been the fabled break. But Elida suddenly panicked over how unhappy Valery was in high school and decided schools in Minnesota were more nurturing. We moved back. I had to accept the fact that my film career was over. I'd worked steadily and spoken a line or two, given many a meaningful glance, tripped villains, sucker-punched heroes, spilled coffee on or skimmed around movie stars in revolving doors. I had appeared in dozens of films, TV episodes, commercials. But Elida hadn't been doing well, and both of us got better, more reliable jobs back home.

Elida loved the minuscule: the hundreds of tiny decisions that together produced a great flow of scenes. She applied this love of detail to her new vocation, planning corporate events. I also loved the small, when it consisted of learning to say lines a dozen different ways, with different tonal qualities, inflections, and gestures. In my new job, as a fund-raiser for a vibrant local theater company, I perfected gestures and tones that I hoped would coax money to my organization.

For my birthday that year, perhaps to console me for the life I'd given up, Elida somehow managed to clip and splice together a half-hour movie of my bit parts, which she set to eerily repetitive music. Shortly after she gave me that gift, which she titled *Man of a Thousand Glimpses*, we parted. I moved out of our downtown condominium, near nurturing DeLaSalle High School.

For the first couple of months after leaving Elida, I bolted out of work at exactly 4:00 p.m. I drove to my tiny apartment impatiently, hungrily, addicted not to a new relationship but to sleep itself. Deep rest was a drug. Waking from relaxed oblivion, I vibrated with an almost tear-inducing pleasure. Why shoot up, I wondered, when just by depriving the body of uninterrupted sleep for twenty years you can have ecstasy with no side effects? Except, it might be said, for Laurene.

It took no time at all before I was sleeping the entire night beside a woman whom I fear I had married too quickly because she slept like a drunk kitten.

From the beginning, I had to consciously keep myself from referring to Laurene in casual conversation as 'my current wife.' Though it was taken as a joke, I knew better: it was a slip. Laurene Schotts was the daughter of the owner of an immensely successful midwestern sporting-goods chain with outlets in the ex-est of the exurbs throughout the tristate area. She was a lover of the theater arts. At the gala dinner for my theater company, which Elida organized pro bono the year we parted, Laurene spoke between the salad and the entrée. Her flattering words of thanks to our supporters, which screened a plea for still greater largesse, impressed me with their genuine, awkward grace.

Laurene reveled in that sort of gala, where people bid on donated items—the use of time-shares in warm countries, fur coats, ski packages, signed books, hand-painted scarves. Scarves draped our chairs and we took superb vacations. Laurene was blond, social, generous, and loved to barbecue. Elida was dark, wayward, introverted, frugal, and usually a vegetarian. Laurene could drink a bottle of cold pinot gris between five and six p.m. Elida might sip one murderous, snore-inducing glass of cabernet between eleven and midnight.

After the divorce, Elida and I met once a month to discuss Valery. We had agreed to do this early on, even when it hurt to see each other. Every time, after we had wincingly established where Valery's college tuition would come from, and whether she needed a new therapist, after Elida had drunk a glass of wine the color of old blood, then confided the latest news of Valery's boyfriend, who we both hoped would turn out to be simply 'experience,' we could conclude the hour with an expansive goodbye, perhaps saying, 'That wasn't so bad after all!' or even 'Good to see you!' We laughed in relief. We hugged, patted each other on the back, sometimes drank a cup of tea for the drive home. We never kissed, not even on the cheek. Our divorce had been agreeable and final. Our postmarital meetings were lingering, tedious, and self-congratulatory.

Once Laurene and I married, however, the meetings with Elida became more difficult. The boyfriend had turned into a problem—we suspected an addiction. We also began, without any warning, to fight. It would start with some obscure thing and progress to even more obscure things. By the end of our meetings, Elida and I were worn out. Then, after one particularly difficult session, still upset as we were saying goodbye, Elida, instead of hugging me, stuck out her hand. I took her hand and held on to it until she met my eyes. Her glare pulled me to her, and I shocked us both by kissing her studious, pale lips. We jumped apart, as though scorched, and turned away. We didn't speak of it.

OUR NEXT MEETING was set up by email, and I found myself walking eagerly toward Nick's, a restaurant off Loring Park, quiet and decorous by day, with leather booths and gauzy curtains that let in glowing white rafts of winter light.

Elida was sitting at the third booth in, and raised a hand as I entered, then put a tissue to her eyes. She had been crying, a rare event. It usually meant, frighteningly, that she'd had some breakthrough realization about me that she'd repressed for years. Warily, I asked her what was wrong. She told me that Valery had started snoring. Her boyfriend had already left her, thank goodness, but Valery was convinced that snoring was the reason I'd left her mother.

'Of course it wasn't!'

'Maybe not. We had other issues.'

'Who doesn't? Twenty good years. One bad year. A thousand little issues came home to roost.'

'I thought, you know, because of those good years, we might get back together,' Elida said. 'Until Laurene. She doesn't snore, right?'

I admitted as much.

'Ah.' Elida turned to look out the window, and her dark glinting hair swung sorrowfully alongside her cheek. 'The first time we spent the night together.'

'Laurel Canyon.'

'I warned you I snored. I had already been to the specialists and had surgery, which only made it worse. It's almost a relief to sleep alone now. At least I'm not blasting a man out of bed.'

'I never minded.'

I thought of the couch in Los Feliz that had wrecked my back. The walk-in closet with a floor pallet in our Minneapolis condominium. I'd adjourned to these lonely sleeping venues on most nights. I did mind, but her fixed gaze shook my heart.

'Last month you kissed me.'

'I did.'

We grew perplexed, ate in silence, each secretly examining the other's face from time to time. I was very conscious of the drama of the situation. Any former actor would have been. Elida sussed that out.

'You're trying on expressions,' she said, laughing.

It was true. Various expressions crossed my face, but none felt right. The elements wouldn't meld. My eyes would express affection while my mouth was tense. Surprise would lift an eyebrow while my upper lip worked cynically. Embarrassment smote me. At least that was real. I put my face in my hands and tried to breathe, but my hands covering my mouth made me hyperventilate. When I looked up, Elida was signing the credit-card slip. She folded her napkin.

'Don't get up,' she said. 'From now on, let's do a phone call. Or text.'

'I really hate texting for personal stuff,' I said. 'Please sit down. We can solve this.'

She sat down. Irrationally elated, I ordered a bottle of wine.

'This is a bad idea,' said Elida.

'Why? We can talk. How are the Ripsaw and the Welders?' Elida knew my nicknames for her mother and sisters.

'Ha!' She clinked my glass. 'What was I again?'

'The Polisher.'

'I don't really mind that,' she said. 'It's in my line of work, really. I miss you. Maybe we should have an affair where we see each other only by day but never sleep together, you know, at night.'

She was speaking whimsically, but we proceeded to do exactly that. We were extremely happy for ten months. To be sure, I felt bad about lying to Laurene, but she noticed nothing. She made few demands, seemed happy enough with my company, and continued to barbecue, even in December. Meanwhile, Valery had left for college, and Elida and I were meeting in our old condominium, overlooking the poisoned brown waters of the Mississippi.

THEN ONE AFTERNOON we were dressed, sipping tea, looking out at the river, when Valery dropped her suitcase inside the door. She was astonished to see us sitting there. She gaped silently for a moment, then clumped down the hall in her big snow boots.

Elida gave me an oddly insolent look. You can live with a person, have an affair with a person, and still suddenly see an unfamiliar flash, like the sleek side of a fish in the shallows, there and gone. She had known exactly when our daughter would arrive home.

Valery screamed when she saw the tousled covers on our bed, the scattered pillows. She clumped back into the living room.

'How long has this been going on?'

We told her. She began to sob.

'All this time? How selfish! Mean! I could have had you both together. Instead, I've been trying to get used to you apart. I was accepting the facts and then . . .'

She pressed her mittened hands to her temples as if to keep her head from flying apart. We all started crying, and, for a while, felt miserable. Then Elida absurdly snorted and we burst into hysterical laughter.

It was decided that I would come clean and leave Laurene Schotts. Elida and I would remarry. It would happen before a justice of the peace and Valery would be our witness. In spite of that strange look Elida had given me, our togetherness gave me an enormous sense of rightness. Things were falling into balance. My elation continued all the way back to Laurene's and my house on Interlachen Boulevard, in Hopkins, facing the golf course. A beautiful stone house, with creamy painted walls, a wet bar on the lower level, and a wall-sized screen for movie-viewing parties. Sitting in my car gathering courage, looking up the flagstone walk, I thought of the pallet on the floor of the condominium's walk-in closet. I would regret leaving the lavish, comfortable house bought with Laurene Schotts's money. There was nothing wrong with

Laurene, either. She was kind, transparent, always well intentioned, and I would regret the silent comfort of her presence every night. I would miss her slumberous body drawing me down into perfect rest.

Laurene pitched a majolica vase, then a framed photograph of us in Peru. She threw a few other breakable objects at the wall and, at last, hefted a crystal unicorn she'd had since the age of ten.

'You'll regret throwing that,' I said. 'Please don't. I'm so sorry!'

'Dad was right!'

Tears rolled down her face, onto her collar, wetting her throat.

I was stricken. I couldn't stop apologizing. Never before had I seen her truly upset or sad.

'Dad was right,' she said again. 'He said you were after the money. He didn't trust you—a former bit-part actor. He begged me to make you sign a pre-nup, but I said, "No, you're so wrong! He's the one!"'

Because I had little money, and because money hadn't figured into my first marriage, except for the problem of not having it, I was until that moment unaware that this had even been discussed. I put it out of my mind and didn't think about it until a month later. I had moved out of Laurene's house into a tiny studio apartment. I continued to see Elida only during the day. I wasn't quite ready for the condominium's walk-in closet.

'Are you crazy?' Elida said, putting down her teacup one afternoon, after I'd told her the proposed terms of my divorce. 'That family is worth over a hundred million! You could get a settlement. They'd never even miss it.'

I waved her off, but every time I thought how handy, how fantastic it would be to have money, I wavered. With my nonprofit salary, I could barely afford to soundproof Valery's old bedroom. I told myself I'd keep my pride and sleep on the closet floor. I'd walk away without a cent. But I didn't.

WE BOUGHT THE condominium next door and removed two walls. This gave us an easy path into a large room, where I set up a huge screen. Before it, we arranged several couches of immense size and comfort. I slept there in grateful quiet. I didn't take Laurene for that much, comparatively speaking, and the Schotts family was relieved. Still, they hated me enough to threaten for a while to get me fired.

One night, Elida surprised me by playing the montage of clips that she'd made for my birthday years earlier. It was worse, somehow, seeing it on that giant screen bought with Laurene's money. There I was, my trivial works captured for the ages. I hadn't noticed, when I first viewed the movie, that Elida had made of those fleeting cameos and set pieces a sort of narrative.

Man of a Thousand Glimpses started out with crowd scenes, me here, me there, the nice-looking, unobtrusive bystander reading a newspaper, glancing up at the sound of a gunshot, the man crossing a street, exiting a bakery, jumping into his car, uncoiling a hose to water his lawn. Next, a better man appeared, somewhat older, more heroic: I ran toward a river with a child in my arms; I was a soldier dragging his buddy to safety; I lowered a dog in a basket from a burning building, addressed people through a bullhorn, rushed into waves, and dived toward despairing arms. After that, I became a good father, inflated bicycle tires, opened refrigerator doors, lay back smiling in my late-night-shopper's easy chair, had my waist measured, drove several cars of screaming kids to supposed sports matches. Small wonder I then got a pounding headache, clutched my jaw, my leg, my heart, wincing in agony. Next there came a turning point, which had been much applauded at the first viewing: I smoked a cigarette in a cheap motel, a beautiful woman silhouetted in the shower behind me. Afterward, ruined, I poured myself drink after drink, ordered a third martini, fell off a barstool, crawled under a table and licked a woman's ankle. I sank even lower—stuck a gun in a teller's face, took cash from the drawer of a fast-food register. I palmed an apple from a pile, stole a moped, a diamond bracelet, a newspaper. These crimes kept me tossing in bed. I stared at ceilings, my eyes luminous, hollow with glare, haunted by ghosts, by women, by hallucinations. Sleepless, I got clumsy. I was hit by a car, crushed by a falling girder, devoured by a live volcano, axed, mauled, invaded by bubonic plague. I was identified several times, in liverish-green morgue light, by stricken, dignified women. It was shocking the way I just kept on dying, physically, then mentally. A wreck of a man, I leaped from a bridge, a window. I parked on train tracks and drank deeply from a flask. I smiled at the glare of swiftly approaching lights and laughed soundlessly.

The End.

Elida left. I played the movie over and over. How dark was my narrative! Why had Elida killed me off instead of letting me rescue dogs in the end? This downward trajectory gave me a moral chill. I decided that I had not only wasted my life but acted ignobly in taking money from Laurene. Although Elida and I had made Valery happy, and I'd thought I was contented with Elida, I knew now, as I'd known before, the nature of Elida's true feelings for me.

I destroyed the movie. It would be years before anyone noticed my long-ago birthday gift had disappeared and I was once again dispersed into the confetti of B movies, failed TV sitcoms, clumsy commercials. No one would ever have the cruel patience to assemble my life glimpse by glimpse again.

WHEN THE HOLIDAYS came around, I insisted that we stay at the house in Golden Valley. Why not? I had already counted a million holes in a million ceiling tiles.

The first night at Elida's parents' house, we all had a mirthful, loving dinner, then did the dishes together. Elida's relatives had easily absorbed me back into the family, where my role, though peripheral, was also vital, because I was Valery's father.

After we turned in and Elida fell asleep beside me, I lay on my back waiting. It usually took her an hour to really get going, but her sisters and her mother had already begun. Valery and a girl cousin had sneaked a bottle of wine into their sleeping bags and were now drifting off next door.

The real snoring hit with abrupt ferocity. The orderly, mechanical regularity of the metalworking shop had been abandoned. Now it was more like a pack of wolves snarling over a kill. I closed my eyes. On my mental screen I saw lions driving the wolves—or hyenas, maybe—into the veld. On a hill overlooking the bloody feast, a baboon whooped. For many hours, I elaborated on the vivid images that accompanied the soundtrack: a lioness worrying the leg off a carcass, two others fending off a male, raking his ribs with teeth and claws, while their cubs mock-fought nearby. At last, I dropped off.

In the deepest part of the night, I woke. Although Elida's snarls had calmed to the loud, gurgling purr of a big cat digesting prey meat, I came to in a sick sweat, shaking. Perhaps my imagined scenario had triggered some terror from my evolutionary past. I had dreamed that I was the hunted animal, thrown to earth, being eaten alive. The tearing of my flesh, the snap of jaws wrestling at my bones, the blissful lapping of the cubs as my throat opened— all this seemed absolutely real to me. It took some time for me to understand that Elida's body had not been satiated on mine, that she wasn't purring because she'd swallowed my heart.

AMELIA

There was excitement when the first Kentucky Fried Chicken franchise opened in Tabor. Now we had something the rest of America had. This was around 1970. No sense that this was the beginning of the end of our character as a town. Anyway, I applied for a job. When I tell people that working for the Colonel paid for my college education, they think it was the job. But that wasn't it, exactly.

I was a server taking orders from behind a glass case that was regularly clouded with grease, from both our fingers and what collected from constant molecular precipitation. The job didn't pay as well as actual waitressing because nobody tipped, but it was not as stressful or demoralizing. There were only a few things to remember on the menu. Chicken this and chicken that. A few side dishes. The night cook, Marty, was friendly to me in an exhausted way. He had pale brown hair that stuck out all over as if he'd chopped it off randomly with a knife. He had a pitted complexion, a paunchy slouch, dark bags under his eyes. He would lean against the back-door frame, blowing smoke into the alley, waiting for the heavy round slugs on top of the pressure cookers to spin. Marty seemed to enjoy hating everything around him, giving a sardonic twist to repeating the orders. 'Large bucket' became 'Laaahge. Fuhhk. Id.' It was a very weak joke, if it even rose to the level of a joke. But I always laughed because then he'd use what seemed his last bit of energy to pretend-surf over the slick tiles to the row of pressure cookers.

Right before closing, Marty always made sure to fry an extra batch of chicken that we'd keep warm in the Heatilator. Of course we couldn't possibly sell it all. We were allowed to bring the leftover chicken home, which made up for the lack of tips to a small degree. I was the oldest of five, three of them boys, and a family with active children can eat an almost unlimited amount of food. I was proud of my ability to add to our larder. Marty brought chicken home too. I think it was all he ate.

One night shortly after I began working, as I stood in fake expectation behind the counter, already bored, an unusual person came into the store. He swung a polished black walking stick as he marched down the aisle between the red and white booths and tables. He was dressed in a white suit and his shirt was white. His hair was white. He wore a goatee and a black string tie. He looked pretty much like the Colonel himself, even wearing the same style of eyeglasses. The man stepped up to the counter and ordered an all-dark-meat dinner, which came with coleslaw, mashed potatoes, and gravy. Shavonne was working with me and took his order. She didn't react to anything about him.

'What's going on?' I whispered to her after he paid for his dinner box and carried it, with a medium Coke, over to a booth by the window.

'You haven't seen him yet? He's just a weirdo. Dresses up like the Colonel to get attention.'

I looked more closely and recognized the man as Mr. Ponath. He was one of the three or four Black people living in our town. Or he was part Black, the way people then said of me, 'She's part Indian.'

'Your heritage is not immediately evident,' one of my tenth-grade teachers had told me. I told my mother, who laughed and said, 'Where's the cheekbones?,' which was what people said to her. Our family has round, friendly faces. This 'not immediately evident' thing was pretty much the same with Mr. Ponath. I suppose like me his grandparents had lived in the area, and their heritage was pretty much evident. People kept track.

Mr. Ponath sat alone for just a short time. Another diner carrying a dinner box came over, sat down, and began to talk with him. Over the next month, I noticed that people approached Mr. Ponath every time he came in. He never ate alone. Sometimes he even ordered an extra dinner and pushed it across the table to someone he seemed to have observed was underfed. I was glad that even though Shavonne thought he was a weirdo, Mr. Ponath had a lot of friends. His costume seemed to be a joke so widely shared that people sometimes addressed him as Colonel. I was gratified by the Colonel's popularity because at school I was classified as a weirdo. I hated eating alone, which I did at lunch most days because I was a rung below the unpopular group. I was unpopular all by myself. But Mr. Ponath gave me hope.

I'd started working in the summer and as fall turned cold, Mr. Ponath drove a large boatlike Buick to the franchise. It was a well-shined maroon car. I learned from my parents, who knew Mr. Ponath as 'tragic,' that he'd bought the car thinking that he would travel around exploring the national parks with his sister, Amelia. She had often taken care of his house when he had to leave for some conference, and it was thought they might travel together once he retired. However, Mr. Ponath had had a terrible shock. Amelia had contracted brain fever on a cruise to Australia. She had walked off the ship and so was lost at sea. He'd been alone now for almost two years and although he had plenty of money, people surmised that he didn't have the heart to pursue the dream of travel on his own.

Now Mr. Ponath's outings were modest. Sometimes he went no

farther than the overgroomed cemetery at the edge of town. During the bout of depression he suffered after his sister's death, he had purchased a plot and a stone carved with his name, leaving the date of his death blank. The stone was surrounded by dark pine trees, whose lowest branches were lopped about eight feet off the ground so that young people couldn't smoke cigarettes or use drugs there. Mr. Ponath went to visit his own grave sometimes, people said, but he perked up once he started dressing as the Colonel.

My mother was always one for sharp observations. Once, she had noted that every time Mr. Ponath left Tabor to visit another town where there was a good bakery to sample, or to Fargo where there was a mall and a downtown theater that played three movies at once, he returned agitated and disturbed. Then he would begin to question people minutely about the time he'd been away. It was as if he'd missed out on something crucial and important, even though he knew that wasn't true. My mother thought it was because Mr. Ponath's family had been here for a few generations. She explained to me that his Black great-grandfather had come to the area around 1870 to garrison at the Dakota reservation, and he had married into the family of a nearby rancher. For a couple of generations, most members of his family had become farmers, but Mr. Ponath had gone to the university and become a professor at our local two-year college.

When I started working, we hardly ever saw the boss, Bob Bjornson. Suddenly, in the fall, he began to come in every night. He started ostentatiously closing out the till, counting the money over and over, acting suspicious of me although the count was never off. Occasionally, Bjornson even worked behind the counter—to keep his hand in, as he put it. 'I know where he keeps his hand,' said Marty with a double raise of his eyebrows. Marty had to stop frying extra chicken of course and to my disappointment there were only a few shriveled pieces to take home now at the end of the night. Shavonne began to criticize the way I wiped down booths and she made me do the vacuuming. But I traded her the vacuuming for making coleslaw, a job she hated and I loved. There was much made of the Kentucky Colonel's secret ingredient, and as far as I could tell it was sugar. There were glittering white cups of sugar in everything, but in the coleslaw dressing there was an extra-impressive amount. Along with the vinegar it just tasted delicious to me. I became addicted to the coleslaw instead of the chicken and began to smuggle tubs of it home in my purse.

One night there was a staff meeting at which Bjornson announced that Shavonne would conduct a 'cleaning seminar' for the rest of us. Marty looked pained, rose slowly, and said he needed a cigarette. He slouched out the door and never came back. At the cleaning seminar, Shavonne gave each of us a toothbrush and indicated the corners of the bathroom that mops couldn't reach, and the ends of the refrigerated cases' sliding tracks that needed toothpicks to dislodge bits of gunk that had collected there. She also brought a little spackle tool to show us how she scraped gum from the bottom of the tables. All of this cleaning weighed on my spirit and I missed Marty's cheering sardonic slothfulness. But things got worse, for then came winter and the deep true cold. The term 'wind chill' wasn't widely used yet. Nor had down coats or polar fleece been invented. I had about a mile to walk and pulled on corduroy pants underneath my uniform, which helped. But sometimes I had to lock up at nine and there is nothing that keeps you warm at -30 in the dark except running. I had to run hard not to freeze.

On a typically cold night, I was standing behind the restaurant's glass door steeling myself for the run, when Mr. Ponath drove up.

I'd talked to him about running home that night and now he offered me a ride. My parents would have picked me up, but it would mean getting the family car started, warmed up, and then out of the garage. A lot of fuss. I knew that I could make it, but I was relieved to climb into Mr. Ponath's warm car. After that, he regularly came in late and stayed on, drinking coffee, which he said relaxed him. Every night, he drove me home in his big comfortable car. I found out more about him during the short drive—what grew best in his garden (peas, strawberries); I heard about his love of the main college course he taught, plant biology. I learned that Mr. Ponath had let his garden go after his sister died but he babied his houseplants. He belonged to the Columbia Record Club, fossil-hunted in the Badlands, hiked in Minnesota, and at one time had owned a canoe.

At the same time that I was learning about Mr. Ponath, things at work were getting worse. The new cook was like Shavonne, very gung ho. He recited Bible verses instead of smoking. His neatness put me off. He had glossy brown hair and rosy skin, roan freckles all over his eager square face and on his arms. Every time I called in an order through the window, he bounded forward, bright-eyed, with an open mouth. When I didn't respond, he shook his head and walked away, miffed at my silence. Did he expect me to say something more? I had the feeling he was watching me all the time. He was. He asked me to go out with him. I said no.

'Someday you will,' he said with a sneaky glare.

'Never!' I cried, as in a melodrama. He was insufferable. Tears sprang to my eyes.

Shavonne saw me put a pint of coleslaw in my purse and she ratted me out to Bjornson. The next evening, he asked me to sit down with him in one of the booths. When I told Bjornson that the coleslaw was from the bottom of the big tub, about to go bad, and would have gone to waste, he said that from now on he wouldn't cause temptation. He'd check the tubs himself and throw out what was getting old. I knew that he'd do no such thing. He'd just mix the old slaw into a new batch. I imagined this mixture poisoning Mr. Ponath and tears came into my eyes again.

'You know you have a fifteen percent discount on food purchased here,' said Bjornson. 'You can always buy your coleslaw if you like it that much.'

'I need the money for other things,' I said, as though taking what he said seriously.

'I've heard your family's always hard up,' he said with fake sympathy. 'I'm so sorry.'

I froze with shame, but just for a moment.

'We're saving because we're all going to college,' I told him. 'Which is more than you ever did.'

His mouth fell open and his neck turned red. 'Shavonne tells me that nobody likes you,' he said. 'I can see why.'

I was pierced through, but Marty's words came to my rescue. 'I can tell where your hands have been,' I said.

'You're fired,' he answered.

I got up and went back to the employee room. I signed a paper Bjornson thrust at me, put on my coat and boots, then marched down the center aisle.

'Where do you think you're going?'

'Home.'

'If you leave now, you'll forfeit your paycheck.'

'You just paid me,' I said and tried to walk through the door. He was there with another piece of paper that I assumed barred me from the premises.

'I wouldn't dream of it anyway,' I said, glaring into his face as I scrawled my signature.

———

THE WIND DROPPED down my neck and poured up my skirt. But Mr. Ponath was just arriving for his evening of coffee drinking and I tapped on the window of his car.

'I just quit. Or actually I got fired.'

I felt a fleck of happiness. I'd been fired! And after I told Mr. Ponath the story, he was not in the least judgmental; he shrugged it off, told me to get in, and he drove me home. When we got there, he said he needed someone to clean his house and organize things. He asked if I would like the job. He told me what the job paid. It was twice what I made selling chicken dinners. I said yes. When I told my parents that I'd accepted a cleaning job with Mr. Ponath, my mother gave my father one of her typically impassive looks that signified a secret trove of meaning. He pursed his lips. They both looked back at me, each waiting for the other to speak.

'Mr. Ponath is a confirmed bachelor,' my mother said.

'Confirmed?' I said in a cheeky way. 'Did the bishop slap him the way he slapped me?' I don't know how Catholic confirmations work now, but we were tapped on the cheek as we stood before the bishop. This tap was to signify the blows we would suffer for our faith. For some reason, the bishop gave me a resounding slap, shocking even himself, and I'd reacted by blurting, '*Ow!,*' cracking up the congregation. It had become a family joke.

'Haha,' said my mother. 'Confirmed bachelor. You know what I mean.'

I immediately suspected this was code for something else, but my father was the more innocent of my parents and took what my mother said at face value.

'I wouldn't say he's solidly confirmed,' said my father. 'He's known to squire women around from time to time at square dances. But he was close to his sister. He took her loss hard. He's lonely.'

'Not really,' I said. 'He has a lot of friends. He never sits alone.'

This surprised them a little. I realized that I hadn't even told them that Mr. Ponath was the person driving me home. They hadn't noticed. I had been leading a secret life, which elated me.

'Make sure he keeps his hands to himself,' said my father in a firm voice.

I thought of Marty's remark but it had already gotten me fired.

'I will. Don't worry. He's not like Bjornson.'

I was astonished at the sudden rage that suffused my father. He bolted half out of his chair. My mother's eyes narrowed and she asked what I meant.

'It's just a rumor,' I said. 'Nothing happened to me. But I did have to clean the base of the toilet with a toothbrush.'

'That doesn't seem very sanitary,' said my mother, 'as you were also handling food.'

'We used plastic gloves.'

She got a gleam in her eye and I feared that my chores at home might include cleaning with a toothbrush. I was sorry I'd said anything.

'I'm safe with Mr. Ponath. Don't worry. And he's going to pay me twice what I made at Kentucky Fried.'

They still didn't seem convinced.

'Cash,' I said for some reason.

My father raised his eyebrows and turned his mouth down. My mother said, 'Still, if he ever gets handsy walk right out.'

The next day, I began working for Mr. Ponath. His house was easy to clean because everything was already put away. Clothing was in the closets, dishes in the cupboards, books on the bookshelves. Mr. Ponath did not collect newspapers and magazines and he went through only half a loaf of bread per week. The rest he threw out. At home, we quarreled over the ends, and I hated to let the bread go to waste. I asked if I could take home his leftover bread and told him that I was surprised to see how long it took him to eat a box of cookies. He encouraged me to help myself. It was a shame he only bought vanilla wafers. After school on Wednesdays I vacuumed, and on Saturday and Sunday afternoons, I dusted, mopped, and cooked the only recipes I knew—hamburger soup and tuna casserole. After my work was finished, we'd play mock vicious games of pinochle and cribbage. He'd drink a large glass of water and a small glass of wine. I'd have tea. When spring came, I made iced tea. I tried to learn new recipes. Because the Colonel had developed a heart condition, he'd given up fried chicken and in fact was trying a meatless diet. These were the days when if you told someone that you didn't eat meat the other person would ask, 'Does that include chicken?' I had some trouble finding vegetarian recipes and made a lot of three-bean salad.

Mr. Ponath thought up special tasks for me, like reshelving books or sweeping out the basement or the garage, which were both clean anyway. Every so often he would ask me to check his sister's clothing for moths. Apparently she'd kept quite a lot of clothing at his house, intending to move in with her brother at some point. After her unexpected death, Mr. Ponath hadn't had the heart to get rid of her things.

This was the first house I'd ever spent much time in other than my family's. And I'd never examined an adult's clothing, let alone a deceased woman's, so this task fascinated me. Amelia's bedroom overlooked the backyard and alley, which was shaded by four red pine trees, tall and stately, unusual in the town. The room had an attractive daybed with a flowered spread and plump square pillows. There was a sewing machine for repairing clothing, curtains, towels. There was a rolltop desk in which, as with the rest of the house, everything was neatly kept. Envelopes in one aperture, postcards, stamps, writing paper. The drawers held files of letters and a few souvenirs. There was a beautiful pearl-handled letter opener. After I had dusted the outside of the desk, I always looked inside because the orderly contents gave me such pleasure.

Amelia had hated the smell of mothballs, so her closet was lined with panels of aromatic cedar. The hangers were also made of cedar. So opening the door released a clean, sharp woodland scent that braced and comforted. It was a living smell. In the closet there were two heavy winter coats, six or seven tailored woolen suits, the waists wide but nipped in, the lapels curved or trimmed with cord, all in shades of brown or blue. There were jaunty fall jackets of wool plaid. My favorite jacket had large square Bakelite buttons, a rich deep yellow, like a duck's beak. There were a few hats, kept in hatboxes, plain fedoras trimmed with bright curling feathers.

ONE DAY I opened a drawer and found a framed photo of Amelia, who resembled Mr. Ponath, only with lush hair, bold makeup, and a small swatch of fur tucked inside the collar of the plaid jacket I was caring for, the one with yellow Bakelite buttons. The picture had been taken at the local photography studio. I quickly shut the drawer. But I grew agitated. Sometimes this prickle of selfish curiosity came up in me. From time to time, I'd want to know everything. I'd open my mouth and make an untoward remark, even an unkind observation. I would surprise myself, embarrass myself. But I couldn't predict when I'd do these things and so couldn't help them from happening. I tried holding in the prickly feeling, though I felt it poking from the inside. One afternoon, I couldn't hold it in.

'So Amelia,' I said. 'Why was she so mysterious?'

'That's out of left field,' said Mr. Ponath. He didn't speak for a while. Heat rose in me, shame at having revived his loss. At last, he spoke quietly. 'Amelia wasn't so mysterious at all. She was my sister.'

'Where did she live?'

'Decorah, Iowa. She played cribbage with me. To win, I might add, not like yourself.'

I tried to keep myself in check, but something goaded at me. I couldn't help myself.

'Do you have any secrets?'

'Yes, I do.'

'What are they?'

'If I told you, they wouldn't be secrets. I like my secrets. How would you like it if I asked you to tell me your secrets?'

I thought about pilfering fried chicken and coleslaw, and shrugged. He gave me a sharp glance, and I had a slipping sensation, as when you lose your footing in a pond. Instantly, I regretted what I had asked. I feared he knew secrets about me that I was unaware of myself.

'I'm not old enough to have any secrets yet,' I said.

He looked at me and shook his head. 'Oh, you will.'

I don't know why, but this made me happy.

We kept playing. During the game I slipped in a question. 'Were you and Amelia twins?' He waved his hand and said they were, then he won, as usual. We started playing again and I asked, 'Identical?' He muttered something. Finally I said that I had thought of a secret. He sighed and leaned back in his chair. I had already complained a lot about Bjornson, but now I told him how Bjornson was just putting the new coleslaw in with the old coleslaw. Some of the coleslaw could have been in the tub a year.

'Now, that's a secret,' said Mr. Ponath. 'Good to know. That stuff could kill you.' He raised his eyebrows and smiled, reminding me of Marty. We talked of Marty and his slovenly but principled attitude. When I lost, we put the pegs back into the little aperture on the side of the board. I said goodbye and went home.

THAT EVENING, MY parents were away at their bridge night and the usual battle had surged up between my brothers and sister, where the younger ones were chasing the older one in and out of our bedrooms. My sister was trying to control them, I stepped in, and as sometimes happened we all suddenly began a ridiculous war. We raged back and forth through the house, overturning furniture, my sister and I grappling with the boys, tossing one onto a bed, holding another hostage, laughing and yelling with joyous fury. I slipped away and used their distraction to run myself a bath. Once the boys discovered where I was, they began to bang on the door and swear they were going to wet their pants.

'You're boys,' I called, serene in the tub. 'Pee outside.'

'Mom said to stop that.'

'Be stealthy,' I ordered.

They were caught in the act just as Mom and Dad came home, and they told how I'd ordered them to pee outside. My mother reproached me.

'I only wanted to take a bath. Is that too much to ask?'

'How many baths do you think your father and I get to take?' asked my mother. I looked from one parent to the other. I hadn't been aware of them taking any baths at all.

'I don't know,' I said. 'You're secretive.'

They burst into laughter. 'Secretive! We're secretive!'

But they actually were quite secretive. They had to be in order to have any life other than the one devoted to us.

———

STILL, ONE THING I'd wondered about when we'd first met was answered, by my job at Mr. Ponath's house. He wasn't a colonel. He was a corporal. I saw his World War II uniform with its two-bar insignia. This might have been meaningless to Mr. Ponath, but I was elated because I was the holder of a secret. I told no one about it.

WALKING INTO THE movie theater to see *Beneath the Planet of the Apes* one evening, I saw Marty coming out. He looked exactly the same, which to me was proof that Kentucky Fried Chicken hadn't caused his greenish pallor and sunken eyes. He asked me about the old place of employment and I told him, proudly I guess, that I'd been fired. He became animated and told me that if I'd been fired, I could claim unemployment. Some extra money would be a nice addition to my college savings, I thought, so the next day I went to the state employment agency, which was quartered in a small brick building that had once been an optometrist's office. I told a skinny, pale, sneering woman behind the desk that I'd been fired. She wore her white-blond hair in an ominous bowl cut. She held up her finger, as if to shush me, though I wasn't going to speak.

'There's not much,' she said. 'I can maybe get you on at the chicken plant.'

If I took that job, I knew I would never in my life eat another piece of chicken.

'I'm going to look for a job,' I said. 'But I was fired, so don't I qualify for unemployment?'

She made an officious gimme gesture with her hand. 'Name.' I told her my name. She went to a file cabinet and removed a file. 'Read your papers. You're not eligible.'

Amelia

The form that Bob had thrust at me to sign as I was leaving said I'd quit of my own volition. I walked back out of the state employment agency. I'd been accepted at several schools we could not afford. How stupid was I? Maybe too stupid to go to college. Maybe (as Shavonne said) I just did well on tests and lacked an ounce of common sense. She and Bjornson were surely at this moment laughing together over a bucket of fried chicken. I pictured them and thought, I have to get out of here. Marty came to mind. I could end up like him, drained and hopeless. I loved my hometown, I loved my family, and the Colonel. But this betrayal by Bjornson made me desperate to leave. I moped along in cold spring rain. When I walked into our house, my father beckoned me into the kitchen. He and my mother sat me down at the table and told me that Mr. Ponath had offered to pay for my college tuition plus room and board.

'We went over this before, but I just have to ask again . . .' said my mother. She left some dots hanging in the air.

'Ask what?'

'Sometimes elderly men get too fond of young women in a way that's just not right,' said my father.

We had indeed been through this before and I had a question ready.

'You mean like Mr. Miller?'

'What? That man you used to wave at? The shut-in?'

'He invited me in. He could walk a little, you know. He tried to corner me and kiss me.'

Again I'd spoken thoughtlessly and upset my parents. Their mouths were open, their eyes wide with indignation. My father looked as though he was ready to rush out and break the old man.

'You'd have to dig him up to punch him,' I said, my prickles coming out. 'Anyway Mr. Miller never got me! I pushed him over! And it's not like that at all with Mr. Ponath. He's like a grandpa to me. Someone helped Mr. Ponath go to college and he became a professor. He just wants to help me because someone helped him.'

They gazed at each other searchingly for so long that I wondered, incongruously, if they were in love. I doubted it, because they had too much to think about with my rampaging brothers. They turned to me and one of them said, 'We still can't let you take his money.'

IT WAS DECIDED, in their minds at least, that I could go to the local college. However, I accepted the most expensive college. If it took me years to make enough money to pay my way through, so be it. I went back to the employment agency and scored an evening job, at the movie theater. For a while, I didn't have time to work as often for Mr. Ponath, but one night I slipped on the steps going down to the basement to clean the butter machine. I dislocated my shoulder and showed up on Mr. Ponath's doorstep with my arm in a sling. He was just coming out the door dressed in his Colonel outfit.

'Can't you go somewhere else for dinner?' I asked. I was a little upset to see him in his outfit, returning to the scene of what I considered a crime by Bjornson. He said I should get some sort of compensation for my arm, and also that we should celebrate me getting into college. We would go to a supper club, where he could get a highball and I could get a 3.2 beer. This was incredibly grown-up. I must say, we had a wonderful dinner. I ordered shrimp for the first time in my life. After we had polished off our food, he looked at my plate and asked what I'd done with the tails.

'Tails? I ate them.'

'Oh no. You have *got* to go away to college.' He laughed.

A week or so later, a scholarship opened up for me. At the same time, my parents went to the limit, paying more than we could afford. They had to relent and Mr. Ponath was to pay the difference. And so it was, I went off and began the phase of life that everyone tells you to enjoy because you will never be so free again.

WHILE I WAS in my third year of college freedom, at the end of winter term, my mother wrote to tell me that Shavonne had married our boss, Bjornson, and that Mr. Ponath had died. I couldn't have cared less about Shavonne, although that explained a few things. I couldn't catch my breath after reading about Mr. Ponath. I couldn't speak, couldn't think. I was haunted by my last visit. During winter break, I had worked for him again, taking care to examine the suits and sweaters and dresses for moth holes, replacing cedar strips and tissue paper, dusting the tops of wardrobes, washing floors, and vacuuming carpets. At one point I'd decided to take everything out of the closet and wipe it down from back to front. There were shelves in the very back that I hadn't worked through yet. I'd opened a hatbox and there, nestled in tissue paper, I had found a soft, luxurious wig, beautifully styled. I could tell it was expensive. It reminded me of Amelia's hair, but when I opened the drawer where the photograph had been, to check, the picture was gone.

I put everything back and went downstairs to wash the painted vases and gilded plates, swishing them in warm, soapy water, drying them with soft dish towels. Then I played cribbage with Mr. Ponath and talked to him about my college courses. I had told him about how my life was bigger—to my joy, it turned out that my sharp comments were appreciated elsewhere. I was the type of person who made friends in college. I'd thanked him many times.

I didn't feel that I'd neglected Mr. Ponath, but after the letter I missed him and mourned his death. Tears were always close to the surface, and I was sadder than my mother imagined. In the letter she made it clear that I hadn't been expected at the funeral. But if not me, I wondered, who? Still, I told myself maybe it had been for the best that I had not had to leave college during finals. I didn't know, then, how a sorrow deferred does not dwindle away but deepens. My consolation at the time was to picture myself bringing flowers to the spot where Mr. Ponath had intended to be buried.

But when I finally came home and showed up at the cemetery with my grocery store bouquet of two roses and six daisies, there was no sign of disturbance at the grave, and the space was still blank on the headstone that was to bear Mr. Ponath's date of death. I found out that Mr. Ponath had left his body to science and no instructions for his burial. His sister had improbably returned, not lost at sea after all, and she'd arranged everything. His house had been sold and all of its contents had been carted off. Yet he had also thought of me— there was still money for me to finish out my college education, even enough to start me on a higher degree. That he'd thought to do this filled me with diffuse anxiety.

I went to the funeral home and found out how to have the date cut into the stone. I wanted to retrieve and bury what was left of Mr. Ponath after science was finished with him, but there was some confusion about how to do that. I wanted his ashes, anything, even the ridiculous string tie. I asked where the objects were that had been taken away, all the things I'd cared for and knew so well. My mother said they were probably scattered around, although many of them had certainly been bought in lots by estate dealers. There was an antique mall in Fargo, so I went there.

The classrooms in an old high school were set up as antique and vintage shops, each with a designated color, era, theme—collections of baseball memorabilia, ceramic dogs, blue willowware, comic books, and games. There were dove-gray hats and hand-stitched gloves. There were plaid jackets with the sort of Bakelite buttons I'd cherished, but none of them were Amelia's.

I walked away. It was too much. Who knew the exact duck's-beak yellow of Amelia's buttons? Who would remember except myself? There were gilded plates and saucers painted with birds, like the ones I'd washed but not them. There were cribbage boards—I opened the special hollows on their sides and counted the pegs. Every so often as I flipped through shoeboxes of old photographs, I would stop, put my hand on my heart, and allow myself to have a terrible, unfamiliar emotion. I wanted so badly to find Amelia Ponath. I wanted to find that very portrait. I began to paw though the old pictures, rushing madly through the faces of the dead. What I felt was a kind of love, or anyway responsibility, that leaves its owner bewildered and aching for words.

AT HOME THAT night, after my brothers and sister had gone upstairs to squabble, I stayed at the kitchen table and started asking questions.

'Did you know Amelia?'

'Who?'

'Mr. Ponath's twin sister.'

'Oh, her. Not very well. I think her aunt raised her. And of course she visited Mr. Ponath. He talked about her, anyway, or we'd always ask him about her. It was tragic how she fell off the cruise ship and ended up on a jungle island fighting for survival every day.'

'But at least she did survive!' my father said. 'Tough cookie. She ate giant clams.'

'She'd been planning to move in with him.'

'Really? She came to make arrangements after he died, but she was very busy. She had to travel such a distance that she even missed the funeral.'

'Did she . . . wait.' My brain began to assemble things—the lovely wig, the photograph that made Amelia look like an identical twin, except fraternal twins can't be identical, the body mysteriously 'left to science.'

'Did anybody actually see them together?'

'People saw Amelia downtown. She liked to shop. She went to church.'

My father cleared his throat and looked bored with this line of questioning. He went out to the garage.

'But did anybody see them together?'

'I don't know. He'd come back. She'd leave. What are the mad housers doing up there now?'

An irregular thumping intensified, and then came a roar of approval or call to arms. I felt my mother had been about to tell me something, but because of the distraction I'd have to lead up to it all over.

'Oh god,' she said, jumping up.

I left the house and went on a walk. There were always quite a number of people out walking early in the evening. I knew almost everyone and knew that my parents would ask who I'd seen out and about. I passed Mr. Ponath's house. All the lights were on, upstairs and downstairs, the shades were up, and I could see people moving from room to room. A party was taking place. I stopped. People burst out of the front door and lighted cigarettes. A side door opened and emitted a flow of music, strumming guitars, ukeleles, voices in harmony and one weird high heart-stopping vibrato that rose and fell. My heart tightened and I felt a warm lift of excitement. I walked in and asked to see the owner of the house. A solid-looking woman with bright black eyes and bleached hair came over to me. I introduced myself and told her that I'd worked for the former owner, Mr. Ponath. Then I asked whether they had bought the house from him.

'No, we bought it from his sister.'

'Amelia?'

'Yes, do you know her?'

'Of course,' I said. 'I'm looking for her address.'

'So are we. Our Christmas card came back just yesterday.'

'From where?'

'Yucatán. A little place on the beach, that's where we sent the card.'

I was keenly disappointed

'I guess she had a sense of adventure,' I said.

'Come on in,' the woman said. 'You look like you want a beer.'

I wandered around with a beer in my hand. I didn't recognize a thing, but I was surprised to see that the food table was dominated by several buckets of the Colonel's finest. I glanced around and there was Marty, looking antsy. I caught his eye and he tipped his head toward the back door. I followed him.

Outside on the back steps, he pawed his front pocket for a smoke. We sat in the friendly silence of old chicken-slinging history, watching the blue-black sky, the stars coming out one by one, winking through the red pines.

'You know, Bjornson sold out,' said Marty. 'I'm managing the place for an owner from out of town.'

My brain whirred.

'Not Amelia Ponath.'

'Yes, her.'

'So you know Amelia.'

'Strange duck. But really, she's the perfect boss. Only checks in by phone every couple months. Has an accountant who handles all the money. Pays me pretty good.'

I bummed a cigarette off Marty and after a few drags decided to let the whole thing go, just go. Otherwise my life would be like Bjornson's way of mixing the old coleslaw in with the new coleslaw. I stood, thrust my cigarette in the air. 'I want to eat life every day! Not be afraid of every mouthful. Not think about every bite!'

'What the heck?' said Marty.

I told him about Bjornson's coleslaw, and he said that everyone already knew.

'People think old Ponath died of coleslaw. He bought a pint the day before he croaked. That's why they sent his body to the medical school.'

I sputtered out some sort of reaction. I didn't say it, but I was filled with admiration at how Mr. Ponath, or Amelia, managed all of this. 'Did they ever, you know, get a toxicology report?'

'Other people got sick. Not real sick, but sick enough. I heard about it. And rumor is Bjornson paid somebody off when it came to testing the body, which science then lost. Nobody would eat there anymore while Bjornson owned it, so he sold the place. Cheap, too.'

I felt my heart swell. Could it be? Had Mr. Ponath meant to take revenge? A mean boss isn't trivial. A sarcastic boss marks a young person's life and Mr. Ponath understood.

I suddenly missed Marty's slothful but generous style of cooking. Whatever else, he hadn't food-poisoned the town. Marty and I walked back in and came out with several pieces of chicken on our paper plates.

Amelia

'To Amelia,' said Marty, lifting a drumstick.

'Amelia.'

They say revenge is a dish best served cold, but it wasn't true in the case of the drumstick. One thing I knew. Someday I'd get a letter from an extraordinary place. The letter would be in Mr. Ponath's handwriting. And it would be signed *Amelia*.

THE STONE

Her family drove north every summer to stay on the end of an island in cold Lake Superior, and it was there that she found the stone. It wasn't on the beach, where stones are usually found, but in the woods. She was wandering in the brush behind the cabin, uncurling ferns, kicking up leaves, snapping the heads off mushrooms. She sat down beside a birch clump and after a few moments her neck prickled. She had the distinct feeling that someone was staring at her. Looking around, she saw the stone. It was black and rounded, nestled in the crotch of the birch clump. Water had scoured out two symmetrical hollows, giving it an owlish look, or a blind look, or, anyway, some quality that was oddly attractive. At first, she was startled and a little spooked, but then she ran her hand over the stone and it felt like a normal stone. It was about half the size of a human skull and perfectly smooth. The girl's mother called to her, and she got up, holding the stone, and carried it into the cabin. At first, she put it beside her pallet in the bedroom she shared with her siblings. But then, thinking that her brothers or her sister might take the stone, she tucked it right at the bottom of her sleeping bag. That night, her feet rested on the cool curve of the stone, and she brushed the smooth eye sockets with her toes.

After a month, the family got ready to return to the city, and the girl put the stone in her backpack, which she kept at her feet for the whole long drive. She did not let anyone else handle her pack, and when she got home she went straight to her room, took the stone out, and set it on her nightstand, where there was also a digital clock and a pile of books. She was old enough now to say good night to her mother and father before entering her room. They did not sit by her bed to read to her anymore. She took her own laundry downstairs as well. Her mother was not the type to go through her children's rooms often, or to clean for them, so school had started by the time her mother noticed the stone.

She mentioned it at dinner. "That rock by your bed looks like it came from the island. Did you find it there?"

The girl nodded, but her mother's remark gave her an uneasy feeling, and that night she put the stone in the bottom of her least used drawer. As she fell asleep, she could picture it, nestled among the summer T-shirts and shorts which would not be disturbed all winter. She was happy knowing that it was there, and for months the drawer seemed the best place for it. She might have kept it in the drawer indefinitely, if it weren't for something that occurred at school.

THERE WAS A boy named Vic, who often acted up in order to get attention. One day, during art class, the girl felt a little tug at the end of her ponytail, and looked around to see that Vic had used his art scissors to snip off a piece of her dark hair. He dangled the lock from his fingers and grinned at her. But she said nothing. She was frozen, staring at her hair. He started to hide the hair, but she found her voice and told him to drop it. She snatched the lock as it left his fingers and balled it up in her fist. At this point, the teacher noticed that something was going on and asked the girl what was in her hand. When the teacher saw the hair, she said that cutting your own hair was the sort of behavior most children had outgrown long ago, and she would have to write a note to her parents.

Her mother was mystified. "Why did you do that?"

Her father lectured her about the beauty of hair.

That night, she put the little clump of severed hair into one of the empty hollows in the face of the stone. As soon as she'd done this, she was flooded with a sense of peace and relief. The entire incident ceased to matter, though she had been terribly upset by it before. She breathed out and laughed as she closed the drawer. It was nothing at all.

After that, whenever something happened to upset her, the girl would go to the stone. She would sit on the bed with the stone in her lap, stroking it, until her agitation subsided. As she got older, in the most difficult of times, to calm herself, she would take the rock into the bathroom with her and set it on the edge of the tub while she soaked. One night, as she lay in the hot water, she became acutely aware of the stone. The smooth, empty scoops in its face seemed profoundly interested in her. A gentle, thrilling ripple spread through her body. After a while, she took the stone into the water with her and held it on her chest, then slid it down her body until it rested, heavily, between her legs. There was the weight and pressure of the stone and the heat of the water. She put her hand on the stone and pushed against it. Then she put the stone back on the side of the tub and closed her eyes.

THE BOY, VIC, made the varsity basketball team; in fact, he was a starter, and the most popular girls followed him home. One night, however, he called the girl, and asked her to go out with him. She did. They went to a movie, and in the darkness he took her hand. His palm sweat unpleasantly, but she did not move her hand, although she wanted to. Later, he drove her home in his family car, which had a child's car seat in back and smelled of peanuts and other food eaten while driving. He parked the car outside her house and bent toward her. His breath was hot and he panted like a dog, she thought, but she put up with the kissing. He took a strand of her hair between his fingers and whispered something into her ear. He said that she was different from all the other girls, more loyal, because she'd never told on him for cutting her hair with his art scissors. She, too, had never forgotten the incident. Gently, she tugged her hair from his fingers.

She got out of the car, walked into the house, and called out to her parents that she was home. She was the oldest of four children, and the others were asleep. Her parents slept downstairs. The house was quiet. Something rustled in the drawer where she kept the stone. She opened the drawer quickly, but there was only the stone, its eye sockets calm. Everything was understood. She slept that night with the stone beside her, and every night after that, too.

Before she went to college, the girl would hide the stone immediately upon rising so that nobody in her family would notice it. But in college, there was no need. She had a single room. And anyone who noticed the stone on her pillow considered it an interesting, even artistic, sort of sleeping companion. Much better, for instance, than the childish stuffed animals that so many girls affected, or the giant stuffed footballs or beer kegs that could be bought at the college bookstore.

But one girl saw the stone and thought it a pretentious sort of thing to do. Sleeping with a stone—how artsy-fartsy. There was some envy, perhaps, of a girl so self-sufficient (though pleasant, smart, musical, organized, sociable) that all she needed to sleep with was a smooth black rock.

Basalt, the girl corrected, whenever her stone was mentioned, which the other girl—Mariah was her name—found so infuriating that one night she picked up the stone and carried it off. Just stole it. She put the stone on her highest bookshelf, above her bed, and waited to see what would happen. That night, the stone fell off the bookshelf and struck the bone around her eye, causing an orbital fracture and maybe a concussion, as she forgot where she was and could not speak for several hours. During the chaos of the incident, the girl picked up her stone, tucked it under her blouse, and carried it back to her room.

The Stone

Again, she had to hide it. She kept the stone hidden for a long time as she continued in her education, perfecting her musical skills.

SHE BECAME SO proficient at the piano that she gave concerts and was hired by an orchestra in a large city. Now she carried the stone to every rehearsal in a leather bag and set it beside the piano. She carried it to every concert as well. She became known for this eccentricity, for sweeping onstage in an elegant, low-necked, black velvet gown with a black leather bag, which she deposited beside the piano before she played. And then, one evening years later, the black bag was not with her. She was such a remote and yet vulnerable person that nobody wanted to question her, but there was certainly some curiosity. The bag did not return, and it was guessed that the orchestra director had at last forbidden it. People forgot. The woman had no other peculiar habits. Her playing was the same as always, perhaps a bit improved.

What had happened was that the stone and she had quarreled. Or perhaps that is not exactly the right word. It began in the bathtub one night, right after she lifted the stone, as usual, to the side of the tub and closed her eyes. Her hand was perhaps too relaxed. She dropped the stone on her knee. Tears sprang to her eyes, not so much from hurt as from betrayal, and she lifted the stone out of the water roughly and shook it. Then, rising from the bath, she smashed the stone down on the bathroom floor. Basalt is hard, but so is ceramic tile. It all depends on the angle of impact. The bathroom floor was only chipped, but a piece the size of a baby's fist sheared off the stone, destroying its strange symmetry. The spell was broken. It was like falling out of love. As she had before, the woman put the stone, now in two pieces, into a drawer she rarely used. Then she dialed the number of a man who had been hounding her for months.

They married. She tried to pretend that she was not a virgin, but he could easily tell and was inexpressibly moved. Her piano playing was now filled with such emotion, in addition to her precision and clarity, that she was invited to tour Europe. She took her husband and left her stone behind.

A STONE IS, in its own way, a living thing, not a biological being but one with a history far beyond our capacity to understand or even imagine. Basalt is a volcanic rock composed of augite and sometimes plagioclase and magnetite, which says nothing. The wave-worn piece of basalt that the woman had slept with for more than a decade was thrown from a rift in the earth 1.1 billion years ago, which still says nothing. Before she broke it and dumped it at the bottom of a drawer, the stone had been broken time and again. It had been rolled smooth by water and the action of sand. Because of its strange shape, it had been picked up by several human beings during the past ten thousand years. It had been buried with one until a tree had devoured the bones and pulled the stone back out of the ground. It had been kept by a woman who revered it as a household spirit and filled its eyes with sweetgrass. It had been shoved off a dock, dredged back up with a shovel, deposited in a heap. It had surfaced in a girl's left hand. A stone is a thought that the earth develops over inhuman time. It is a living thing to some cultures and a dead thing to others. This one had been called *nimishoomis*, or 'my grandfather,' and other names, too. The woman had not named the stone. She had thought that naming the stone would be an insult to its ineffable gravity. And yet once she had broken it, she set it casually in a drawer with old belts, unmatched socks, pilled sweaters, and stretched-out bras. She had left it there and gone off with a man named Ferdinand, who'd always hated his name and went by Ted.

The Stone

Ted could feel her pulling away from him, gradually, and so gently that it was a long time before he understood that while he'd been adjusting to each tiny, incremental motion, she'd been shifting entirely. By the time he saw things clearly, she had turned her back on him. It wasn't on purpose. She didn't know that she was doing it. He couldn't point to any evidence in their day-to-day life. She was never unkind. She was always attentive, thoughtful, even loving. But there was a glassy distraction. He could feel it, though he could not describe it in a way that made sense.

By this time, her concerts were few and far between, and she taught at a local institute for music. She and Ted had moved back to the city and inhabited the same apartment, now a condominium, half of an old house in a bucolic part of town. There was a large yard, with plenty of birds, a nearby park. What should have been a pleasant life, however, became painful because of this invisible distance. It took a few more years, but eventually Ted understood that he didn't want to live with a simulacrum of intimacy. He left, and the woman wept over him, until at last, to restore her balance, she decided to clean the house and opened the drawer where she'd put the two pieces of the stone.

There are glues that can join stone to stone so well that the seam can hardly be detected, and the woman used such a glue to fit the stone back together. This was one thing that had not happened to the stone before. Now only the thinnest line told the story. The woman placed the stone on a sunny kitchen sill, and felt so well that she began to cook a nourishing dinner for herself. She chopped fresh basil and garlic—as much as she wanted—and dripped olive oil into a saucepan. Then she put the stone in the sink and poured olive oil over it as well. The pores of the stone soaked up the oil. Whenever the stone looked dry, from then on, she oiled it. When the stone looked bored, she carried it to the window, so that it could watch what was happening in the trees.

At night, when she settled in the golden light of her reading lamp, she placed the stone beside her on an antique piece of embroidered linen. She became very old in this comforting life, and in the last few years divested herself of many possessions so that her niece and nephew, of whom she was fond, would not have much to go through after she was dead. She was lucky enough to die with the stone beside her when an aneurysm ruptured in her sleep. As the blood seeped into her brain, she dreamed that she had entered a new episode of time, in which she and the stone would become the same through the endless repetition and decay of all things in the universe. Molecules that had existed in her body would be joined with the stone's molecules, over and over in age after age. Flesh would become stone and stone become flesh, and someday they would meet in the mouth of a bird.

ACKNOWLEDGMENTS

The author gratefully acknowledges Deborah Treisman, who has edited many of these stories. Thanks also to the publications in which these stories originally appeared, in slightly different form:

'Python's Kiss' (as 'Nero') in *The New Yorker*, April 30, 2012.

'The Hollow Children' in *The New Yorker*, November 28, 2022.

'Love of My Days' in *The New Yorker*, June 2, 2025.

'Domain' in *Granta*, November 15, 2014.

'Asphodel' in *Anonymous Sex*, edited by Hillary Jordan and Cheryl Lu-Lien Tan, February 1, 2022.

'Big Cat' (as 'The Big Cat') in *The New Yorker*, March 24, 2014.

'The Stone' in *The New Yorker*, September 9, 2019.

'Love of My Days,' *The Best Short Stories 2026: The O. Henry Prize Winners*, ed. Tommy Orange and Jenny Minton Quigley.

'The Big Cat,' *The Best American Short Stories 2026*, ed. T. C. Boyle and Heidi Pitlor.

Many thanks to Jonathan Burnham for guidance in shaping this book and its visual art. It has been one of the delights of my life to work with my daughter Aza Erdrich Abe, whose art enlarged the scope and meaning of these stories. Miigwech!

ABOUT THE AUTHOR

Louise Erdrich, a member of the Turtle Mountain Band of Chippewa, is the award-winning author of many novels as well as volumes of poetry, children's books, and a memoir of early motherhood. Erdrich lives in Minnesota with her daughters and is the owner of Birchbark Books, a small independent bookstore.

RAISING READERS

Books Build Bright Futures

Dear Reader,

We'd love your attention for one more page to tell you about the crisis in children's reading, and what we can all do.

Studies have shown that reading for fun is the **single biggest predictor of a child's future life chances** – more than family circumstance, parents' educational background or income. It improves academic results, mental health, wealth, communication skills, ambition and happiness.[1]

The number of children reading for fun is in rapid decline. Young people have a lot of competition for their time. In 2024, 1 in 10 children and young people in the UK aged 5 to 18 did not own a single book at home.[2]

Hachette works extensively with schools, libraries and literacy charities, but here are some ways we can all raise more readers:

- Reading to children for just 10 minutes a day makes a difference
- Don't give up if children aren't regular readers – there will be books for them!
- Visit bookshops and libraries to get recommendations
- Encourage them to listen to audiobooks
- Support school libraries
- Give books as gifts

There's a lot more information about how to encourage children to read on our website: **www.RaisingReaders.co.uk**

Thank you for reading.

---

[1] OECD, '21st-Century Readers: Developing Literacy Skills in a Digital World', 2021, https://www.oecd.org/en/publications/21st-century-readers_a83d84cb-en.html

[2] National Literacy Trust, 'Book Ownership in 2024', November 2024, https://literacytrust.org.uk/research-services/research-reports/book-ownership-in-2024